Off Season

ORCA
YOUNG
READERS

Off Season

ERIC WALTERS

Book #6

ORCA BOOK PUBLISHERS

Library and Archives Canada Cataloguing in Publication

Walters, Eric, 1957–
Off season / Eric Walters.

ISBN 10: 1-55143-237-4
ISBN 13: 978-1-55143-237-3
(Orca young readers)

I. Title. II. Series.
PS8595.A598O43 2003   jC813'.54 C2003-910199-1
PZ7.W17129Of 2003

First published in the United States, 2003
Library of Congress Control Number: 2003101353

Summary: Nick and Kia are just beginning to get the hang of life in the wilderness when a raging forest fire threatens to destroy Ned's home and cut off their escape.

Orca Book Publishers gratefully acknowledges the support for its publishing programs provided by the following agencies: the Government of Canada through the Book Publishing Industry Development Program and the Canada Council for the Arts, and the Province of British Columbia through the BC Arts Council and the Book Publishing Tax Credit.

Cover design by Teresa Bubela
Cover photography by Laura Leyshon
Interior illustrations by John Mantha / Mantha Designs

ORCA BOOK PUBLISHERS
PO Box 5626, STN. B
VICTORIA, BC CANADA
V8R 6S4

ORCA BOOK PUBLISHERS
PO Box 468
CUSTER, WA USA
98240-0468

www.orcabook.com

Printed and bound in Canada.
Printed on 100% PCW recycled paper.
010 09 08 07 • 5 4 3 2

Basketball certainly isn't life, but if it's played well it can teach some important lessons about life.
Play, enjoy, live!

EW

Chapter One

"Under the 'I,' seventeen."

"Got it!" Kia said as she placed a marker on her bingo card.

"Under the 'N,' thirty-four."

"No good. If she'd call out 'N' forty-four and then 'O' sixty-nine, I'd have bingo."

"Gee, wouldn't that be exciting," I mumbled.

"More exciting than not playing. I don't know why you didn't get a card and play."

"It's just too strange to be playing bingo on an air — "

"Under the 'O,' sixty-nine."

Kia screeched with delight as she marked off the spot. "Just one more number."

"You know what that means," I said.

"Shut up, Nick."

"Every time you get to one number left, somebody else wins the — "

"Shut up, Nick."

"Under the 'B,' seven."

"Bingo!" somebody yelled out from the back.

Kia shot me a dirty look, as if somehow my predicting it had made it come true, and if I'd kept my mouth shut the bingo wouldn't have happened.

"We have a bingo," the announcer — the flight attendant — said. "Please hold onto your cards until the winning card has been checked." She walked past us and down the aisle.

"I hope the prize isn't anything that I really wanted," Kia said.

"You mean like food?" I asked. "What I really want is a meal."

The flight attendant came back up the aisle and picked up the microphone. "We have a winner."

There were groans that echoed throughout the plane.

"And that was our last game," she continued and even louder groans followed.

"Your attendants will be coming and collecting your cards and markers. Thank you for participating in bingo — a game where the stakes aren't high, but where the players are . . . thirty-two thousand feet high."

"This has got to be the craziest airline in the whole world," I said, shaking my head.

"It has been a little different."

"A little?" I questioned. "No movie, no meals, no headphones, pillows or blankets."

"Bargain airlines don't give you the extra things. That's why the flight was so cheap. Besides, I liked playing bingo and that one flight attendant was really funny."

I couldn't argue with that. He had gotten up and given us our safety instructions just before we took off. He then went on to give the "Top Ten Reasons to Fly a Discount Airline." These reasons included "They let you fly inside the plane," "You don't have to worry about what the first-class passengers are eating," and "They can park the plane anywhere because they're not afraid of it getting dented by the other planes' doors."

"How are you two doing?" another one of the flight attendants asked as she hovered over us.

"Good, fine," I said.

Maybe it was a discount airline, but all the flight attendants had been really friendly to us. They took turns coming over and talking to us and offering us drinks of pop — there wasn't a meal on the flight, but they'd provided enough Coke, pretzels and cookies to fill us up.

I guess they really didn't have much choice but to watch us. I'd turned ten in April and Kia's tenth birthday wasn't until September 19 and my Mom had told me that they had to supervise us because we were traveling on our own. Whatever the reason, I found it reassuring. Especially since I really didn't like flying at all to begin with.

"Are we landing soon?" I asked.

"We're going to start our descent within fifteen minutes and be on the ground within thirty."

"We'll be landing?"

"That's usually how we like to end our flights — with a landing," she said and Kia chuckled.

"I guess the only other choices are to either stay up in the air or smash into a mountain," Kia said.

"One isn't possible and the other we don't even like joking about," the flight attendant said.

"Sorry," Kia apologized.

"When we do land I want you two to stay in your seats until the other passengers have deplaned. I'll be escorting you off the plane to meet your party. Who will be waiting for you?"

"Ned and his mother, Debbie," Kia said.

"Ned's my cousin," I explained. Ned was my age. We were even born on the same day, although I was three hours older. We were going to be spending a week with Ned and his parents in the mountains where they lived. His father was a park ranger and he lived and worked in a national park.

"Aren't they your cousins too?" the flight attendant asked Kia.

"Just friends . . . Nick and I aren't related."

"I just assumed you were brother and sister." She paused and smiled. "You seem a little bit too young to be a married couple."

"We're not!" Kia protested.

"Friends!" I exclaimed. "Best friends since we were little."

I was so tired of people making jokes or snide comments about Kia and me being boyfriend and girlfriend or how we sometimes acted like an "old married couple" — my mother had said that about us.

"I should have known you were just friends," the flight attendant said. "If you were married, you would have been fighting over who gets the window seat."

"There's no argument there," I said. I didn't like heights and I wanted to be as far away from the window as possible. I even leaned into the aisle when we took off.

There was a little pinging bell sound and the "fasten seat belt" lights went on.

"It looks like we're preparing for landing," the flight attendant said. She walked away down the aisle.

"Don't be nervous," Kia said.

"I'm not nervous," I lied.

"Flying in a plane is safer than driving a car."

"Flying is safe. Takeoffs and landings aren't," I said.

"What do you mean?"

"Accidents don't happen in the air. They happen when the plane is taking off or landing," I explained.

"We've already taken off."

"I noticed."

"And in ten minutes or so we'll be on the ground."

"That's what I'm counting on. On the ground and — "

The little bell pinged again.

"Can I have your attention please," a male voice requested over the intercom. "We are making our final approach into Kelowna International Airport. The weather is warm, sunny, with a strong breeze from the northwest. It is a perfect day to be on the ground." He paused. "Unfortunately, due to the strong winds, the perfect place to be isn't in the air. We will experience strong turbulence . . . Turbulence is the fancy aeronautical term for bumpy . . . really bumpy."

"Great, just great," I mumbled.

"Raise your hand if you like roller coasters," the captain said.

Kia's hand shot up into the air. I liked roller coasters even less than I liked airplanes.

"I really can't see if your hand is in the air because I'm flying the plane, but those of you who like amusement park rides might be in for a little bonus at no additional cost. Please recheck and tighten your seat belts, make sure the trays are up, your seat is in the fully upright position and try to keep all of your limbs inside the vehicle until it comes to a complete and full stop."

"What did he say?" I gasped.

"He was making a joke," Kia said.

"Why does everybody on this plane think they're a stand-up comic?"

"Hopefully he's a *sit-down* comic," Kia said. "Like sitting down in the captain's chair in the cockpit. Get it?"

"I get it . . . and I was wrong."

"Wrong about what?"

"There's at least one person on this plane who isn't funny . . . you."

"Now you two *do* sound like an old married couple," the flight attendant said as she stood over us once again.

"Prior to landing your flight attendants will go over the safety features of our aircraft and point out the emergency exits. This is required by law and is not an indication of how they feel about my abilities as a pilot."

Kia chuckled. "He *is* funny."

"That's just what I want in a pilot. I can see the headlines in the newspaper — the head of the airline is quoted as saying he doesn't know why the plane hit the mountain because the pilot was 'one of our funniest'."

Kia started to ramble on about me being too negative and I tried to block her out. Maybe it was just a regulation but I really, really did want to be reminded where the emergency exits were located.

"What was that sound?" I gasped. A whirring, mechanical noise vibrated beneath our feet.

"That's the landing gear going down," Kia said. "I heard it's always best to have it down when you land."

At that same instant I could feel the plane

slowing down, and my ears were becoming more plugged up. I chewed harder on the wad of gum in my mouth. The plane suddenly did a little dip and I felt my stomach shoot up into my throat. Maybe not having any meals wasn't such a bad idea. If I did throw up it was only going to be a mixture of pretzels, cookies and Coke. The thought of that particular mix didn't do anything to ease the queasy feeling in my stomach. I reached into the pocket on the back of the seat in front of me and pulled out the airsick bag.

"You're not going to bring up are you?" Kia asked.

"Hopefully not," I said. "I just want to be prepared."

The plane dipped again, this time bigger, and then swung to one side. I gave a little burp.

"That's more like it," Kia said.

I put the bag down on my lap, held onto the armrests tightly and closed my eyes. The plane swayed and rocked and dipped. This didn't seem any better. Maybe my eyes couldn't see what was happening, but my stomach certainly could feel it — and it was my stomach that was causing all the problems to begin with. I opened up my eyes just as the plane bounced and the tires squealed. We'd touched down!

For the first time I dared to glance out the window. The green grass and the cement of the runway whizzed by us. The engines roared as the pilot used reverse thrust to brake, and the scenery started to pass more slowly by the window.

"Welcome to Kelowna!" the pilot said over the intercom. "That wasn't quite as bad as I'd promised — my apologies to those hoping to add a little excitement to their lives. On behalf of the flight crew we thank you for flying with us, and whether you are now returning home or starting a holiday or business trip, we wish you all the best. This is your pilot, Crash Davidson, signing off."

"*Crash* Davidson?" I asked Kia.

"What a cool name for a pilot."

"*Crash*?"

"Yeah. I'm sure it's just a nickname."

"I figured that," I snapped. "But what about all the other possible nicknames . . . things like Happy or Safety or Fly Boy or just plain Captain."

"Maybe they were already taken. But it doesn't matter. We're here, we're on the ground and we're safe, so stop worrying . . . or at least worry about something else for a while."

Chapter Two

"I'm sure they'll be here soon," the flight attendant said.

Our flight had been in almost an hour. Everybody had gotten off the plane, got their luggage and was long gone. Except for the two of us.

"They have a long way to come," I said apologetically.

"Do you know where they live?"

"They live way up in the mountains."

"That doesn't really narrow it down a lot. Most of British Columbia is mountains. Do you know *where* in the mountains?"

"Not really," I replied.

"Maybe we should call them," she suggested. "Do you have a telephone number?"

"No number. They live way, *way* in the mountains. They don't even have a phone."

"Or a TV," Kia said. "Not that that would help us find them . . . I'm just amazed that somebody can actually *live* without a telephone or TV."

"Maybe they had car trouble," I said.

"I'm sure it's nothing serious," the flight attendant added.

"What would happen if they didn't show up at all?" Kia asked.

I hadn't thought about that — I didn't *want* to think about it.

"I guess I'll just have to adopt the two of you. Then you really would be brother and sister."

"Seriously. What would happen?" I asked anxiously.

"I'm not really sure. I've never actually heard of that happening before."

"It's like that movie," Kia said. "You know the one, *Home Alone*. Except this time it would be called *Alone But Not Home*."

The flight attendant laughed. "It's good you can still make jokes about it. If it was me, I think I'd be too worried to laugh."

"Worrying isn't my job," Kia said.

I held up my hand. "That's where I come in. I do the worrying for both of us."

"But what would happen if they didn't come to get us?" I asked. I really did want an answer.

"I imagine we would put you on the next available plane."

"You mean back home?" Kia exclaimed.

"Back home. Your entire vacation would consist of two plane — "

"Nick! Kia!"

I spun around to see Ned and Debbie running across the empty terminal toward us. I dropped my bag and ran toward them. I'd never been so glad to see somebody in my whole life! Debbie threw her arms around me and I gave her a big hug back.

"It's so great to see you!" I yelled. "And Ned it's great to see — " I stopped mid-sentence as I looked over and up at Ned. "You've grown. . . more than before!"

"Growing like a weed!" his mother said. "Or should I say a beautiful flower!"

Ned started to turn red — which perfectly matched his hair. The last time I'd seen him — last summer — Ned stood head and shoulders above me. He had been like the world's tallest nine year old. Now he had to be close to six feet tall, which of course made him the tallest ten year old in the known universe.

"And Kia, dear, how are you?" Debbie asked as she gave Kia a big hug too.

In my rush of relief I'd temporarily forgotten about her.

"I'm fine," Kia said. "Just glad that you're here."

"We're all glad you're here," the flight attendant said.

"I'm so sorry we're late," Debbie said.

"That's quite alright. I'm just grateful that you're here and everybody is okay. Now I should get going. Bye, kids, and I'll see you in a week."

"You will?" Kia asked.

"Our crew is working the flight back."

"All of you?" I asked.

"The whole crew," she said.

"Even the pilot?"

The flight attendant gave me a questioning look.

"I think he's a little nervous about your pilot . . . his name."

She laughed. "I guess Crash isn't the best name for a pilot, but believe me, it has nothing to do with the way he flies."

"That's good to hear," I said. "So I guess we'll see you in a week."

"Take care," she said and she started away across the terminal.

"And we should be going too," Debbie said. "It's a long way back home."

"How long?" Kia asked.

"Around five hours."

"Our flight wasn't even five hours!" Kia exclaimed.

"If the car is acting up it takes even longer, so the sooner we start the sooner we get home."

"Did you have car trouble today?" I asked.

Debbie looked at Ned, who was looking down at his enormous feet.

"Not car trouble as much as trouble in the car," she said.

She continued to look at Ned. He looked up. "I was carsick . . . a few times."

"So we had to pull over, clean up a little and let Ned's stomach settle before we went any farther," Debbie explained.

"Ned, were you reading in the car?" I asked.

He nodded his head. Ned always got motion sickness when he read while driving.

"If you know you're going to get sick if you read, why do you read?" Kia asked.

"It's a long drive and it was a good book."

"But why didn't you stop after you got sick the first time?" I asked.

"It was a *very* good book."

16

"And did you finish it?" she asked.

"Just before I threw up for the third time."

"Was it worth it?"

He nodded his head. "Like I said, it really was a very good book."

"So what do you think of the scenery?" Debbie asked.

"It's pretty," I answered.

"And it keeps getting better," she said. "Once we leave the highway and hamburger joints and traffic and crowds behind."

We had been passing through small towns and there were some other vehicles on the road, but I wouldn't exactly call any of this busy or crowded. In some ways it had been a little piece of being back home. Sure there were no mountains in the background where we lived, but both places had the same drive-through restaurants lining the road.

"And just smell the air!" Debbie said.

Their big four-wheel-drive truck didn't have any air conditioning — "bad for the environment" — and the air was rushing in through the open windows.

"Doesn't it smell wonderful?"

"Sure," I mumbled, although the odor I could still detect had more to do with Ned being carsick than it did with the mountains that surrounded us.

"It's a shame that Kia is missing all of this."

Both Ned and Kia were sound asleep. Kia was tired because she'd been so excited about coming that she'd been up half the night. Debbie had given Ned something so he wouldn't be carsick, and that often made people sleepy.

They'd been asleep for over two hours, barely making it out of the airport before drifting off. On the downside, I would have liked some more company. On the upside, Ned being asleep pretty well guaranteed that he wasn't going to get carsick again.

"Ned's been so excited about you and Kia coming. He's been counting the days," Debbie said. "I remember when there were over 187 days to go."

"187?" I questioned.

"Christmas day. The Christmas card your parents sent us confirmed that you were coming. We let Ned see the card on Christmas morning. He said that was like a Christmas present, except better than any of the real presents he got."

"He said that?"

"Even more than his telescope, and he's wanted a telescope for years," she said.

I was starting to feel guilty. I'd agreed to the trip last summer, but as the time got closer I tried to figure a way out of the whole thing. I liked Ned, and he was family, but I didn't like the idea of leaving everybody and everything behind for a week and traveling to the other side of the country. That's when my mother got the idea of Kia going along with me. That made everything better . . . or at least alright.

"Ned has so many good memories of last summer. He said that spending time with you and Kia and winning that Hoop Crazy tournament was one of the highlights of his entire life."

"It was pretty exciting," I agreed.

Ned, Kia and I, and Mark, another one of our friends, had entered the NBA-sponsored three-on-three contest. Kia, Mark and I had been teammates on our rep team for years, so we knew how to play. Ned's only experience was that he could identify a basketball. He'd never played in a game — hardly ever seen a game — and really hadn't even liked sports. Ned liked bugs. No, that was wrong. Ned *loved* bugs — and nature and reading and talking about things that no kid in the whole world cared about. I used to call him Nerd instead of Ned — well at least I called him that when he wasn't around.

That meant that when Ned joined our three-on-three team — a last-minute substitution because we needed another body — he had virtually no skills at all. What he had was height.

Ned was one gigantic guy . . . the tallest kid for his age that I'd ever met or known. Seeing the two of us standing side by side — him towering over me — nobody would ever guess that we were born on the same day. In fact I was actually three hours older.

"Sometimes I worry about Ned," Debbie said.

I wanted to say something about all of us worried about Ned, but I kept my mouth shut.

"I guess it isn't Ned I worry about so much as the way we live."

"What do you mean?" I asked.

"My husband and I love living in the mountains, but it's a difficult life for Ned to be so far away from everything and everybody."

"Ned told me he loved living in the mountains," I said.

"That's what he tells us too. I always wished he had some kids to play with . . . Our nearest neighbor is almost an hour away. How would you like that?"

"I wouldn't," I admitted. "I'm unhappy because Kia and I aren't going to be in the same class next year."

"Why not?" Debbie asked.

"That's just the way they divided up the classes. There are five grade five classes in our school next year."

"That's amazing!" Debbie exclaimed. "I forget about what it's like to go to school in the city." She paused. "Actually, I forget what it's like to go to any school. It's hard when your mother is your teacher and you're the only one in the whole school. I might not feel so badly if Ned at least went to school."

Ned was homeschooled and got his lessons by mail. He was the same age as Kia and me but while we were going to be starting grade five in the fall, he was going to be doing grade seven work.

"That would be better. If he was going to a school, how far away would he have to go?" I asked.

"The nearest school would be a three-hour

drive each way. Could I ask you a question?" Debbie asked.

"I guess so."

"And will you promise me you'll be completely honest with me?"

"I guess so." I had a terrible feeling in the pit of my stomach. This couldn't be anything that I really wanted to answer.

"Do you think that Ned is a little . . . a little different?"

I looked over at Ned. His hair — as red as fire, sticking up in a dozen directions — thick glasses on his face, wearing a T-shirt that read "Science is Happening Here!" his gigantic feet hidden inside his gigantic hiking boots, the only kid I knew who wanted to be an entomologist when he grew up instead of a professional athlete. His head was leaning against the side window of the truck, his eyes were closed, and a little trail of drool was coming out of his mouth and down his cheek as he slept.

"Well?" she asked.

"What do you mean by different?" I asked, stalling for time.

"Different from other kids."

If she'd asked me that question a year ago I would have known exactly what I thought

— Ned wasn't just different, he was weird . . . a Nerd. But now?

"It's okay to tell me what you think," she said.

I looked over at Ned, sleeping peacefully. He wouldn't hear what I said.

"He's different . . . but different isn't bad. Ned is Ned because he is different. If he was like everybody else he wouldn't be Ned."

"But being different can be hard for somebody . . . especially a child."

"It can be," I admitted. "But take Kia for example," I said, looking over at her. She was making a low whistling sound through her nose as she slept. "She's my best friend in the world. She plays rep basketball, she said that only clowns in the circus need to wear makeup, she's confident and nothing bothers her, even when it does. She's different than any other girl I've ever met, and that difference is what makes her not just *better*, but the *best*."

"That is so sweet that you feel that way about her," Debbie said. "You really do care for her, don't you?"

"She's my best friend," I said. It felt okay to say nice things about her because she was sound asleep and wouldn't hear me.

"I just wish that Ned had a friend like you."

"Ned does have a friend like me!" I protested.

"I know that, Nick, and you're a good friend. It's just . . . just . . . *sad* that the kid he feels closest to lives thousands of miles away and he only gets to see him once a year."

I didn't know what to say, but she was right, it did seem sad.

"My husband and I have talked about Ned's need to be around other kids. There's a strong possibility that we're going to move," she said.

"Move where?"

"A few hours away from where we live now. My husband has been offered a post close to a town."

"How close?"

"Close enough that I could drive Ned to school."

"Hopefully he wouldn't read on the way," I joked.

She laughed. "He'd be able to go to school, be with other kids, play with them and make friends."

"That *would* be nice."

"He could even play sports. He's really become quite the little basketball player since last summer."

"I don't know about the *little* part."

"He's always getting me out there to play

24

with him and he's gotten quite good. He beats me most of the time now."

That isn't how I usually define being a good player — "he's even *better* than his mother."

"It would give him a chance to fit in," Debbie said.

Ned . . . a six-foot-tall ten year old who spit out big words like he'd swallowed a dictionary, who was supposed to be going into grade five but was actually doing grade seven work. I thought it would be great for him to be with other kids, but I didn't know if he'd really fit in anywhere.

"Would he be in grade seven or grade five?" I asked.

"I think that it would probably be best for him to be around kids his own age, so we've talked about grade five."

Kia let out a loud groan, opened her eyes and stretched. Thank goodness she was awake. I was afraid that the next question I was going to be asked was if I thought Ned could fit into a grade five class.

"Have I missed anything?" Kia asked.

"Some of the most beautiful scenery in the country," Debbie said. "But the nicest is still to come. Our turnoff is just up ahead.

Which reminds me, I better get gas before we go any farther."

Up ahead on the left a gas station came into view. Debbie slowed the truck down and pulled into the station. Ned's head bumped against the glass of the window as the truck rocked to a stop, but he remained sound asleep.

"Do either of you have to go to the washroom?" Debbie asked. "This is our last formal washroom break until we get to our cabin."

"I'm okay," I said.

"Me too," Kia replied.

Debbie got out of the truck and started to pump gas.

"That was nice," Kia said.

"What was nice?" I asked.

"What you said about Ned."

"But, but you were asleep."

"I *was* asleep."

How much of what I'd said had she heard?

"Ned is different, but that's what makes him special." She paused. "Just like me being different is what makes me the *best*."

I slid down into the seat and felt myself turning red.

Chapter Three

The truck hit another gigantic rut and the only thing that stopped me from hitting the roof was the seat belt holding me in place.

"That was a bad one," Debbie said.

"There's a lot of bad ones," Kia said. "This road is awful."

Calling it a road seemed pretty generous to me. It was a narrow trail cut through the trees. If a car were coming from the other direction, somebody would have to pull right off the road to let the other vehicle pass. Not that that seemed like a worry — we hadn't seen another vehicle, or another human being, for the past forty-five minutes.

When we'd first turned off the highway we'd been on a dirt road. Then after a while we'd turned onto a much narrower road. What we were on now was more like a hiking trail than a road.

"These are the old lumber roads," Debbie said. "The lumber companies cut them out of the forest so they could get in and harvest the trees."

"They let people cut down trees in a park?" I asked.

"That was before this was a park. These trees are all new growth. The real old, big trees were all taken a long time ago."

"These seem pretty big to me," I commented as I looked out the window and up into the trees that came right to the edge of the trail.

"They're not bad."

"Is this the only road to your house?" I asked.

"The one and only. It's actually not bad in the summer. In the winter the snows can be bad."

"Do you ever get snowed in?" I asked.

"Occasionally, but thank goodness this old buggy can plow through the drifts. The worst is in the spring. When the snows melt and the rains arrive, this trail can become a muddy nightmare. Of course that wasn't a problem this spring."

"It wasn't?" I asked.

"We hardly had any snow last winter and there hasn't been any rain to speak of for weeks and weeks. That's why the forest isn't so green."

"This looks pretty green to me." There was nothing but trees and leaves as far as the eye could see.

"Not compared to usual. There are lots of places where the bushes are brown. Everything is pretty dry."

We kept moving along the trail. The truck bumped down hills and lurched up the other side. We passed by streams and curved around little lakes and ponds. It was beautiful. And wild. And far away in the middle of nowhere.

Of course there were no people, but there were animals. Two deer — a mother and a little fawn — had crossed in front of us. There were geese and ducks on the ponds, and eagles soared above us in the skies. A big fat skunk had been sitting up on its back legs on a rock beside the road. If we'd seen that many animals, I could only imagine how many were in the woods and wilds all around us.

"Could you give Ned a little nudge?" Debbie asked.

"That pill really made him sleepy," I said. Other than a couple of brief awakenings and when we stopped for a late lunch, he'd slept almost the entire way home.

"That combined with the fact he has hardly slept for the last two nights," Debbie said.

"Why not?" Kia asked.

"He's just been so excited about you two coming."

"I had trouble sleeping last night as well," Kia said.

I leaned over and gave Ned a nudge. "Hey, Ned, wakey, wakey . . . time to get up."

Ned roused from his sleep. He rubbed his eyes with his hands, stretched and reached for his glasses, which had rearranged themselves onto his forehead.

"How far are we from home?" he asked.

"Boy, are you asking the wrong person," I said.

"Not far," Debbie said.

Ned looked out the window like he was scanning his surroundings. "We're practically there. I shouldn't have slept that long!"

"You obviously needed it. Now you'll be rested so you can stay up late tonight," Debbie said.

"How much farther is it?" Kia asked.

"About that far," Debbie said as she suddenly brought the truck to a stop. "There it is."

I looked out through the windshield — through the film of dust and the dozens and dozens of bug splatters that formed a remarkably colorful pattern. All I saw were more trees.

"I don't see anything," Kia said.

"Down the hill . . . snuggled amongst the trees," Debbie said.

I looked past the bugs and into the distance. There, hidden in the trees, sat a log house. The brown of the logs and the green roof blended in perfectly with the surroundings.

Debbie started the truck in motion again and we bumped down the hill and came to a stop right beside the house.

"Is Dad home?" Ned asked.

"He was due back this afternoon," she said and turned to face us. "He was away on a surveying trip through one of the sections of the park for a few days."

We climbed out of the truck. I stretched my legs and took a deep breath. The air did have something special about it. When Debbie and Ned had been visiting us they'd often complained about the way our city air "smelled." Now I thought I knew what they meant.

"First thing you need to do is check your animals," Debbie said to Ned. "Make sure they have food and water."

"What sort of animals do you have?" Kia asked.

"I'll show you."

We walked around the side of the log house. It was a lot bigger than it looked from the front. We circled to the back. There were a number of large pens, higher than I was tall, made of wood and wire mesh.

"I'll show you my babies," Ned said.

He undid a latch holding the door closed, opened it up and stepped inside. We followed. I didn't see any animals at all and wondered if whatever had been in there wasn't there anymore.

"Cats!" Kia shrieked in delight. "You have cats!"

Two cats came running and bumping and careening across the cage. They ran right up to Ned and bounced against his legs. They were both bawling loudly. He bent down and scooped them up in his arms.

"They're not really cats," Ned said. "They're still kittens really."

"Aren't they pretty big for kittens?" I asked.

"Not for lynx kittens."

"Lynx?"

"A feline species native to this area."

"What are you — "

"They are so adorable!" Kia exclaimed, cutting me off. "Can I hold one?"

"You can hold both of them if you want."

"One is good to start." Kia reached out and Ned handed her one of the cats.

"Do you want to hold one as well, Nick?"

"Sure." I took the second one from him. "Boy, are they soft."

"And they love attention. Give it a little rub behind the ears and see what happens."

I did what Ned suggested. It rubbed back against my hand and started to purr!

"That is so cool!" Kia said. "Where did you get them from?"

"My father is always bringing back animals that he finds abandoned in the woods."

"He just takes baby animals?" Kia asked.

"Not takes as much as rescues. Animals get killed by other animals all the time," Ned said and shrugged. "And some of the animals that are killed are mothers who leave babies behind."

"That's awful," Kia said.

"Not awful. Just nature. If my father didn't find them they'd die. We raise them until they're old enough to take care of themselves."

"And then what?" I asked.

"Then we let them go, back into the woods."

"That must be a sad day," Kia said. "You know, saying goodbye to your pets."

"It's sad and happy. I'm sad to see them leave, but glad that they get to go back to nature because they really aren't my pets. Wild animals should be in the wild."

"That makes sense."

"Over the years we've raised dozens of animals," Ned said. "Raccoons, rabbits, skunks, a porcupine, a bear — "

"You raised a bear?" I exclaimed.

"He stayed with us for about five months. Then he started to get too big . . . he kept ripping through the wire and trying to get into our house to see me."

I looked around anxiously. "Is he still around here?"

"No, he went to a special bear rescue preserve where they had the space and time and experts to help raise him."

"What other animals do you have here now?" Kia asked as she continued to pet the little lynx.

"I have pack rats, a pine marten, a porcupine, a — "

"A porcupine?"

"The next pen over," he said.

"Won't he shoot his quill things at us?" Kia asked.

"He's a porcupine, not Robin Hood," Ned

said. "They don't shoot quills, they loosen them. Besides, he's still a baby so he doesn't even have quills yet. Come on and I'll show him to — "

"Hey! Where's my little Ned?" called out a big, booming voice.

Ned looked up and his whole face brightened. "It's my father . . . he's home!"

Ned rushed from the pen. He hadn't gone more than a dozen steps before he was met by his father who picked him up and swung him around in the air.

Suddenly Ned didn't look so big compared to his father, who was much taller and wider. I hadn't seen him for years and I'd lost track of just how big he was. I couldn't help thinking that Ned was big now, but he was probably going to get a whole lot bigger before he finally stopped growing.

Ned's dad set him back down on the ground.

"Now where's that Nicky?" he called out as he walked toward the pen.

I had a terrible feeling that I was about to be hugged, lifted up and spun around. He ducked and turned sideways so that he could fit through the opening of the pen. With his size and his stride and the full beard covering his face, he reminded me of a charging bear.

At the last second he stopped and stuck out his hand — his paw — to shake. My hand disappeared into his huge mitt.

"Good to see you again, Nicky!" he bellowed as he pumped my arm up and down. "You've grown!"

"A little," I answered. Compared to him and Ned, I felt very small.

"And this must be Kia!" he exclaimed. "Ned was right, you are a pretty little thing!"

I looked over at Ned. He was looking down at those big feet of his and his face was becoming as red as his hair.

"Thanks," Kia said.

"What?" he asked as he turned his head to one side.

"I said, *thanks*," she said louder.

"You have to speak up or at least speak into my good ear," he said. "Haven't heard well out of my left ear ever since I was hit by lightning."

Kia and I laughed.

"He's not joking," Ned said.

Kia and I both looked at each other.

"Sucker seared the hair right off the top of my head, shot down the left side of my body and went out through my left foot . . . blew the shoe clear off!"

"That must have hurt," I said loudly, not knowing the right thing to say to somebody who'd been a human lightning rod.

"Hurt like heck . . . at least what I can remember of it. Woke up face down in a ditch."

"I've never known anybody who was hit by lightning," Kia said.

"Happens to park rangers all the time," Ned said. "There's a guy in the United States who's been hit seven times!"

"Once was more than enough for me, thank you."

"So are you going to be around for a few days now?" Ned asked.

His father shook his head. "I've got to go away to check out Maple Ridge . . . I'll be leaving first thing tomorrow, gone for a day and back by dinner the next."

"I was kinda hoping you'd be sticking around for a while," Ned said.

"Sorry, no can do." He paused. "But tell you what, how about the three of you come along with me?" He turned to Kia and me. "You two feel like a little hike in the woods?"

"Sure," I said.

"Sounds like fun," Kia replied.

"Good. We leave at sunrise tomorrow."

We unpacked and settled in for supper. It was a good meal — a big meal. I couldn't believe how both Ned and his father could put away food. Ned practically licked the serving bowls, cleaning up the last grains of rice and the last of the casserole — the vegetarian casserole. I'd forgotten that Ned and his family were vegetarians. Somehow it struck me as strange that somebody as big as his father wouldn't eat meat. I could almost picture him just picking up a cow and chewing on it. Apparently not eating meat hadn't slowed down his growth.

"So what did you think of my cooking?" Debbie asked.

"It was good . . . really good," I said.

"Yeah, I liked it a lot," Kia agreed.

"Are you two going to be able to go a whole week without meat?" she asked.

"I'm practically a vegetarian," Kia said.

"You are?" Debbie asked.

"Yeah. I only eat animals that are vegetarians," she joked. "Actually, I can live without meat, but I'm not so sure if I can last that long without french fries."

"That we might be able to take care of," she replied.

"You can?" Kia asked.

"I was thinking that we might take a little trip into town in a couple of days. I have some shopping I need to do. Do you have any idea how many groceries I have to buy to keep up with these two?" she said, gesturing to her son and husband.

"I can only imagine."

"Hopefully you're not going tomorrow or the next day," Dan, Ned's dad, said. "These three are coming with me on a little hike tomorrow."

"How far are you going?" Debbie asked.

"Maple Ridge."

"That's a lot more than a little hike," she said. "Do you think they'll be able to manage that?"

"Of course they can," he said. "They're young . . . in good shape if they're playing sports. Shouldn't be a problem."

I hadn't thought it would be a problem until she'd mentioned it.

"How far away is this place?" I asked. "How far are we going to walk?"

"It's about six hours . . . each way."

That certainly didn't sound like any little hike to me.

"Just a little walk in the woods. We're going to leave just after sunrise."

"In that case maybe these three should get to bed soon," Debbie said.

"How soon?" Ned asked. "Couldn't we do something for a while first?"

"What did you have in mind?" his mother asked.

"I was thinking that maybe we could go down to the mall and do some shopping," Kia said.

"Mall . . . shopping? There really isn't any mall around here for a — "

"Ned, I'm joking. What do *you* want to do?"

"I was hoping we could play a little basketball."

"Basketball?" I asked, my ears perking up. "Now that sounds like a plan."

"Would that be okay?" Ned asked his parents.

"I think that would be fine. The three of you go and play some basketball, and your mom and I will clean up the kitchen."

"That sounds like an even *better* plan," I said.

Chapter Four

I picked up the basketball and started spinning it on the tip of one of my fingers. It was a nice ball . . . leather, just worn enough to be easy to handle.

"So where's this court you've been talking about?" I asked.

"Right down the way," Ned replied. "Are you sure you want to play?"

"Do birds fly?" I asked.

"Well . . . the vast *majority* of birds do fly," Ned answered, "but there are many flightless species including ostriches, emu and penguins . . . although many people consider the manner in which penguins *swim* to be much like *flying* through the water and — "

"Ned," Kia said, cutting him off. "He does want to play basketball. Consider him like the vast *majority* of birds."

"So you *do* want to play?" Ned asked.

I nodded my head. Apparently whatever

cool we'd given him had worn out and Ned was once again the Nerd.

"Oh . . . good . . . we should play. Follow me," Ned said and then headed for the back door.

Kia grabbed the ball from me. "Yeah, follow him, unless you're like a penguin or an ostrich or some other big fat bird too heavy to fly . . . or jump and get rebounds."

"I'll show you who can't get rebounds!" I snapped. I reached out to try to take the ball back, but Kia danced out of my reach and out the door after Ned. I ran after her. She and Ned were walking up the dirt trail away from the cabin.

"I'm afraid it isn't in the best shape right now," Ned said. "The creek took off one of the corners."

"The creek did what?" Kia asked.

"It washed away the back corner."

"Washed it away? You mean it isn't paved?" she asked.

"Nothing can be paved or built here without special permission."

"Permission from who?" I asked.

"The Parks Commission."

"You mean like the park rangers? Like your dad?"

"Like my dad's bosses."

"So did he ask them?" Kia questioned.

"No," Ned said, shaking his head. "My father said he's here to protect the park, not pave it. He doesn't believe in disturbing the natural ecosystem."

"What?" I asked.

"He doesn't think anything should be built in the park that disturbs nature. It took both me and my mom to convince him to let me even make a dirt court."

"Just where is this court?" I asked as we continued up the dirt track.

"It's not much farther. Less than a kilometer."

"Why didn't you just put it right by the house?" Kia asked.

"Because there wasn't a spot close to the house. I had to put it someplace that was relatively flat and didn't have any trees. It's just through here."

Ned turned off the dirt track and onto a trail that cut through some bushes — raspberry bushes — like the ones I had in my backyard.

"Have you ever played on a dirt court before, Kia . . . Kia?" I turned around. She had stopped and was searching through one of the bushes.

"Kia!" I yelled.

"I was just trying to pick a few raspberries. You know how I love raspberries!" she called back.

"How about we play some ball and you eat later?" I stood on the path and waited while she caught up to me. Ned continued on along the path ahead of us.

"How were the berries?" I asked.

"I couldn't find any."

"I'm sorry about all this," I said.

"It's not your fault there were no berries," she said.

"I didn't mean the berries, I meant about bringing you along and the basketball court. It'll be hard not to play ball for a week. I didn't know it was just made of dirt."

"Who cares?" she asked. "We didn't come here to play basketball and it wouldn't hurt either of us to have a vacation from basketball for a week. Don't you ever get tired of it?"

"Me get tired of basketball?" I asked, sounding like I couldn't believe what she was saying.

"Come on, be honest," she said. "I'm not your mother."

I didn't answer right away. "Sometimes."

"For me it's toward the end of the season

when we have the playoffs coming up and everybody is taking everything so seriously and I'd like to just sleep in one Saturday morning instead of going to some game or practice."

"Sleeping in would be nice," I admitted.

"So what if we don't even shoot a ball for a week? Who cares? Let's just enjoy the trees and the woods and all this nature stuff, okay?"

"Sounds okay to me."

"Hey!" Ned yelled and I turned around. He was standing, waving, from a bend in the trail up ahead. "Are you two coming?"

"Let's go," I said to Kia, "and no matter what his court looks like, let's just pretend we're impressed."

"Goes without saying."

We caught up to Ned. He was standing on a little rise in the trail.

"So what do you think of my court?" he asked.

I looked past him. There, through the brush and berry bushes, sat a beautiful little basketball court.

"That looks amazing!" I exclaimed.

"It has lines," Kia said.

"All measured out and in the right places. The key, three-point line and out of bounds . . . everything."

"You painted the dirt?" I asked.

"Not paint. Come on, I'll show you."

Ned led us down the trail to the court. I stopped at the outside line . . . It wasn't a line but a thin strip of wood that had been set into the ground to form the line.

"The outside line is made of birch, but just branches that had fallen off or were already dead. We set them into the ground flush so they don't stick out."

"That's amazing."

Kia was already on the court, bent over, examining one of the lines at the key.

"And the lines on the court are made of ground-up chalk," Ned said.

"Like on a baseball field," I suggested.

"Not exactly. This is completely natural and biodegradable so that even when it's washed away it doesn't harm the environment."

Kia started bouncing the ball. "And it's flat, perfectly flat."

"Not perfect, but pretty flat. My father said it's to within three degrees of completely flat. Of course that one corner isn't so good by the creek."

The far corner was obviously sloping down.

"And you built all of this?" I questioned.

"Me and my father. We gathered the wood together and worked to make it flat and marked out the lines and put up the hoop."

The hoop . . . I'd been so amazed by the court I hadn't even noticed the hoop. It was a clear, Plexiglas backboard attached to a tree.

"It's regulation height and we attached it to the tree with special brackets so the tree wouldn't be hurt. So what do you think of my court?"

"It's amazing," I said.

"Really something," Kia agreed.

"And do you want to see something even more amazing?" Ned asked.

He took the ball from Kia's hands and walked over to the three-point line. Slowly and deliberately he set himself and then put up the ball. Nothing but net!

"Way to go, Ned!" Kia yelled.

"That was a great shot!" I exclaimed. And totally unexpected. Ned had only started to play basketball last summer when he joined us for the tournament, and he wasn't exactly what you'd call a great shot. Actually, calling him a bad shot would have been a compliment.

Ned loped over and retrieved the ball. "Anybody can make one shot. Could just be luck."

He put up a second shot and it dropped!

"Two in a row!" Kia yelled.

Ned grabbed the loose ball. "Still could be just a fluke." He walked out to the three-point line again and put up another shot. It dropped!

"I've been practicing my shooting," Ned said. "And reading."

"There are a lot of really good basketball books," I said.

"Not basketball. Math."

"How would a math book help you shoot basketballs better?" I asked.

"I learned about angles and arcs. Shooting is all about geometry."

"And practice," Kia said.

"I did that too."

I took the ball from Ned and started to dribble when I saw something and stopped. Just off to the side of the key there was a gigantic pile of poo. Oh, yuck.

"I think we're going to have to do one thing before we play," I said, pointing out the offending pile.

Ned grabbed a stick from beside the court and began poking at the pile.

"Bear poo," he said.

"You're kidding, right?" I asked anxiously.

"No," Ned said as he continued poking it with the stick. He didn't look like he was trying to move it as much as examine it.

"Judging from the size of the dropping it could be either a large black bear or a semi-mature grizzly, no more than two years of age. There are traces of berries, which either type of bear would eat, but I'm looking for fish bones or the remains of a larger animal that would indicate it was a grizzly."

"So you're saying that a bear, a real bear, was right here on this court?" I questioned.

"How else would you think that the droppings got here?" Ned questioned.

"I just meant . . . oh, forget it," I said.

"And judging from the freshness of the pile, I think it has been here no more than two hours ago."

"Two hours?" I gasped.

"Could have been a bit longer or as little as ten minutes ago. I can't tell for certain. Of course my father could tell for sure but I — "

"You're telling me that a bear was right here where we're standing and it could have been here just a few minutes ago?" I questioned.

"Not a few minutes. We've been here for a few minutes and the bear would have heard us coming . . . you two are very noisy and we were yelling and — "

"Where is it now?" I asked.

"In the forest."

I looked around us. The court was surrounded on three sides by the berry bushes and low brush and by the creek on the fourth. On the other side of the creek there were tall cliffs, topped with trees. Nervously I scanned the brush around us. I didn't see anything. I didn't hear anything. It was quiet. Maybe too quiet.

I pulled the basketball up to my chest like I was trying to protect it or hide behind it or something . . . That was ridiculous! If a bear charged me the only thing I could do was throw it a perfect chest pass.

"Should we be out here?" Kia asked, as always voicing my thoughts.

"Why not?" Ned asked. He sounded genuinely confused as to why she even asked the question.

"The bear."

"Oh, you don't have to worry about him."

"Because he's long gone, right?" I asked.

"Probably."

"Probably?" I asked. That wasn't the reassurance I was looking for.

"It's hard to say for sure, but this time of year bears spend their whole time on the prowl, looking for food. It isn't like he's going to stick around."

"That makes sense," I said. "Besides, I'm sure they're afraid of people."

Ned looked at me in shock. "You think an eight hundred-pound bear is afraid of you?"

"They're not?"

He shook his head. "Afraid is the wrong word. They do try to avoid people when possible . . . especially black bears. If they hear you coming, they try to get out of your way."

"And grizzly bears?"

"Depends if they're hungry."

"Hungry?" I gasped. "You mean they're more dangerous before breakfast?"

Ned laughed. "They're more dangerous in years when the food supply is low."

"And is it low this year?" I asked anxiously.

"The lack of rain means there weren't many berries, so it's not a good year for bears . . . which isn't good for us." Ned paused. "Do you know the way to tell a black bear from a grizzly bear?"

"The color?" I asked.

"Size?" Kia questioned.

"Both of those, but the best way is to look for the hump."

"Hump?"

"Grizzlies have a big hump on their backs. The rule is, if it has a hump, make a lump. If it's black, fight back."

"You want to explain that to us?" I asked.

"Yeah, explain it," Kia agreed.

"If you're attacked by a grizzly — a bear with a hump — you put your arms over top of your head to protect your face and neck. You make a lump."

"And that works?" I asked.

"Better than fighting back. That just gets it mad. So just play dead and hope it eventually gets bored and goes away."

"And if it's a black bear you fight back?" Kia asked.

"You yell and scream at it. You put your hands over top of your head." Ned explained by demonstrating. "That makes you look bigger and the bear will probably run away."

"Forget about the bear running. If I see

a bear, I'll be the one doing the running," I said.

"You can try. You'd be amazed just how fast a bear can run," Ned said.

"You'd be amazed at just how fast *I* can run if I'm being chased by a bear," I countered.

Ned and Kia both laughed.

"But really, if a bear is chasing you, you don't have to be able to outrun it," Ned said.

"You don't?"

He shook his head. "All you have to be able to do is run faster than *one* of the people with you." Ned started laughing at his own joke. I didn't think it was that funny. Especially since I was pretty sure that Kia was faster than I was.

"Forget about running," Kia said. "I'm climbing a tree."

"Oh, yeah," Ned said, "that's the other way you can tell a grizzly and black bear apart."

"How?"

"If you climb a tree and it climbs up after you, it's a black bear."

"And if it doesn't climb up, it's a grizzly?" I asked.

"Exactly. They don't climb trees."

"So we'd be safe up the tree."

"Not really. The grizzly would just shake the tree until you fall out or it falls down."

Kia giggled nervously.

Maybe Ned was just putting us on . . . trying to get the city kids all nervous.

"You've lived here for almost your whole life, right?" I asked Ned.

"Almost all."

"Have you ever been bothered by a bear?"

"Never. Not once," he added.

"That's what I thought — "

"But my father has . . . five or six times."

"He's been attacked by bears five or six times?" I gasped.

He nodded. "But he did the things I told you, the things he told me, and he was fine."

"That's good to know!" I said. I felt better.

"Except for the one time, with the one bear." Ned said.

"Your dad was attacked by a bear?"

"It's something that happens to park rangers. If you want, he'll tell you all about it," Ned said. "He'll even show you the scars."

"Scars?" Kia and I said in unison.

"On his back and arm. I think he needed around one hundred stitches."

I handed the ball to Ned. "I don't feel much like playing basketball anymore."

"Me neither," Kia agreed.

We started to walk away when I heard the sound of a basketball hitting against the backboard. I stopped and turned around. Ned was still on the court, taking shots.

"Ned, come on!" I called out.

"I'm staying to take some shots. You two go if you want. You know the way don't you?"

"Of course," I yelled back.

"Just go back along the trail . . . the one that goes through the berry bushes . . . the berries that the bears like so much."

"He's just joking around, right?" Kia asked.

"Ned isn't somebody with a real sense of humor."

"Or you could just wait a while and I'd go back with you!" Ned yelled.

"What do you think?" I asked Kia.

"Maybe we should just stay here for a while and shoot a few baskets."

Chapter Five

"How you doing?" Kia asked.

"Tired. How about you?" I asked.

"Tired doesn't cover it."

Ned and his dad were up ahead of us on the trail. Kia and I were sort of keeping up, just not keeping completely up. The energy that I'd had for the first few hours had slowly leaked away.

"Do you think we're going to take another break soon?" Kia asked.

"I doubt it," I said. "Ned's dad is like a really, really big version of that Energizer bunny. But I bet he'd stop if we asked him."

"Why don't you ask him?" Kia asked.

"Not me. I think *you* should ask him. He didn't say that I was *pretty*."

Kia shot me a dirty look. "He's your cousin."

"My mother's cousin's husband is what he is, but I'm not asking him to stop."

"Why not?"

"I just don't want to ask . . . I don't want him to think that I can't keep up."

"But you can't keep up. Neither of us can."

"But he doesn't know that," I argued. "Let's just keep going for a while."

Kia let out a big sigh but didn't say anything more.

Ned and Dan disappeared over a rise in the trail. I didn't like that. Somehow the woods seemed less wild when there were other people around. Especially somebody as large as Dan. The biggest thing that kept me going — even bigger than my pride — was the need to keep him in sight. There were lots of animals out here, and while *some* of them were even bigger than Dan, *most* of them were bigger than Kia and me. Having him in sight meant that we were safe . . . well at least safer. I remembered about the bear attacking him. It must have been one really, really huge bear.

"Come on, let's move quicker," I said and picked up my pace to try to get them back in sight.

"I thought you were tired," Kia said. She struggled to pick up her pace to catch me.

I made the top of the rise and Ned was

standing there just over the edge. His father was well down the trail.

"My father wanted to know if you two needed to take another break," Ned said.

"That would be — "

"But I told him you wouldn't," Ned said, cutting me off. "I told him about what great shape you two are in because of all the basketball you play."

"Thanks," I mumbled. It was certainly different going up and down a basketball court than it was going up and down a mountain.

Ned started walking again and we fell in behind him.

"How much farther do we have to go?" Kia asked.

"My dad said we have around two more hours to go."

"But how far do we still have to walk?" Kia persisted.

"That I'm not sure about. Distance and time are different things. I don't know what the trail looks like up ahead."

"Are we even on a trail?" I asked. I'd been wondering about that for a while.

"My father is breaking a trail and we're following behind him, so I guess *technically* we're on a trail."

"This would probably all be easier if we were wearing the right type of shoes," Kia said.

Ned was wearing hiking boots. Kia and I were wearing basketball shoes. I was always wearing basketball shoes. You could never tell when a game might break out — although the odds were very long that it was going to happen out here.

I'd always thought that basketball shoes were right for any occasion — first day of school, wedding, church, going out for dinner, visiting your grandparents. I'd now found the one activity that made me want to have something else on my feet.

I adjusted the strap on my backpack. It had started digging into my right shoulder. In my pack was a sleeping bag, a little thin foam mattress to go on the ground, a few pieces of clothing and some food. Kia had pretty well the same things. Ned had those things plus some pots, an axe and the heads for a shovel and rake — minus the wooden handles. I'd asked him if his father was planning to do some gardening while we were out here, but Dan said they were bringing them along "just in case." He didn't say in case of what and I hadn't asked.

Dan was carrying a lot, probably more than the three of us combined. He had almost all our food, two tents, his sleeping bag, a Coleman stove and assorted other things. He also had a chainsaw strapped to the outside of the pack. It wasn't a big chainsaw, but it certainly looked like it still weighed a lot. I didn't even bother asking why he was bringing the chainsaw along. I figured it was probably "just in case" as well.

Up ahead, Dan disappeared over another rise. I picked up my pace again to get him back in sight.

"So what did you think of my cooking?" Dan asked as we all sat around the stove, our plates balanced on our knees. We were sitting on some logs that Dan had positioned around the stove.

"It was pretty good . . . you know, considering," Kia said.

"Considering what?" he asked.

"Considering those hot dogs weren't made out of meat," she said.

"I got news for you, Kia," Dan said. "*Most* hot dogs aren't made of meat."

He and Ned started laughing.

I took another little handful of trail mix — a homemade combination of nuts and dried berries and other fruit — and stuffed it in my mouth. It was tasty. That meant that either it really was good or I was still hungry. Maybe both. Hiking could really work up an appetite.

"What would be perfect now would be to roast some marshmallows over a campfire," Kia said.

"No marshmallows," Dan said, shaking his head. "Nothing but processed sugar."

"I get bumps when I eat processed sugar," Ned added.

"And even if we had them, we couldn't roast them over a campfire," Dan continued.

"Why not?" I asked.

"There are no open fires allowed anywhere in the whole park due to the dry conditions and the fear of sparking a forest fire," Dan explained.

"I didn't know that."

"The whole place is so dry even a small fire could spread quickly," Dan said.

"That's why we brought along the shovel, rake and chainsaw," Ned added.

"You lost me," Kia said.

"Those are the basic tools you need to fight a small forest fire," Dan explained.

"A chainsaw?" I asked. What would you use that for, cutting up a burning tree?

"The chainsaw, and all the tools, are used to create a fire line . . . a break in the forest cover to try to stop the fire from advancing," he said.

"From that point, if the wind is right, you set up a backfire," Ned added.

Gee, that cleared up nothing.

"It's simple and complicated," Dan said. "Tell you what, Ned can explain it all to you. He's read a lot of books about fighting forest fires."

"Lots."

"So you could fight a fire?" Kia asked.

"I know how to fight them," Ned said. "I've read all about them, but I'm too young to actually fight them."

"Or be anywhere around them," Dan added. "But once he turns sixteen, he can come along with me when it's needed."

"That would be exciting," Kia said.

"And dangerous," I added.

"And with all the dry weather, this summer has the potential to be both exciting and dangerous."

"Have there been a lot of fires?" I asked.

"There've been a lot of fires but nothing

in this part of the park," Dan said. "But that's partly because it's been restricted."

"You mean you have to be eighteen years old to get in the park?"

Dan laughed. "It doesn't matter how old or young you are, you're not allowed into this section of the park."

"Ever?"

"Just until there's enough rain to reduce the fire risk. Most fires are caused by people, so no people, no fires."

"I guess that makes sense," I agreed.

"Matter of fact, that's why we're here. There was a report of some people heading in this direction."

"Doesn't look like there's anybody here."

"Not that I can see, but there's a lot of park. You'd be surprised how hard it is to find somebody in here even if they want to get found."

"And harder if they don't want to get found," Ned added.

"Why wouldn't somebody want to be found?" I asked.

"There are lots of reasons," Dan said, "but if they're here we'll find them . . . tomorrow. We should probably be turning in for the night."

It was starting to get dark. The sun was just visible over the hills to the west of our campsite.

"What time is it?" Kia asked.

"Almost nine-thirty."

"Isn't that awfully early to go to sleep?" she asked.

"Not if you're tired. Are you two tired?" Dan asked.

I nodded my head. I could have practically fallen asleep sitting up. We'd already set up two tents — one for Dan and the other for the three of us. I was looking forward to climbing into the tent, into the sleeping bag and going to sleep.

"Couldn't we stay up for a little bit longer?" Kia asked. "Even though we don't have a camp- fire or marshmallows, we could still do my favorite camping thing."

"What's that?" Ned asked.

"Ghost stories," she said.

"No stories for me," I said. "I just want to go to sleep." I was tired, but even if I wasn't, I didn't want to hear any ghost stories. I never wanted to hear any ghost stories.

"I don't like ghost stories," Dan said.

"Are they too scary for you?" Kia asked mockingly.

Dan shook his head. "It's not that they scare me, it's just that made-up stories can't compare to the real thing."

"What do you mean?" Kia asked.

"I mean that the things that are real are much more strange and scary than any pretend, made-up story," Dan explained.

"Like Bart," Ned said.

"Bart? Bart who?" Kia asked.

"Bart was somebody I once knew and — "

"Dad, you're not going to tell them about Bart, are you?" Ned sounded worried.

"You're right," Dan said. "It probably isn't wise — especially not out here."

"This sounds interesting," Kia said. "Come on, let's hear the story."

"That's it, Kia. This isn't a story. It's true." He paused and took a deep breath. "I guess if I hadn't been there . . . if I hadn't known Bart for fifteen years . . . I wouldn't have believed it myself. But I saw it with my own eyes . . . and I'll never forget."

"Dad, I don't think you should tell this story," Ned said.

"And I think you should," Kia said.

Dan turned to Ned. "They want to hear it," he said.

I didn't know where he got the "they" part from. I didn't want to hear anything.

"You can tell them if you want to," Ned said, "but I'm not going to sit here and listen. I know if you tell the story I won't be able to sleep tonight." Ned got up and went to the tent. I had to fight the urge to join him, but I couldn't. I both wanted to hear the story and didn't want to hear it. My only hope was that maybe Dan would decide Ned was right and he really shouldn't tell the story.

"I first met Bart over fifteen years ago," Dan began, and I knew I was trapped.

Chapter Six

"I remember that day well," Dan continued. "It was a hot summer day . . . very much like this one . . . that I first met Bart."

"I can't help thinking about Bart Simpson," Kia said and giggled.

"Bart Simpson?" Dan questioned.

"From TV," I explained.

"Oh . . . TV . . . I haven't watched TV for at least ten years," Dan said. "Actually his last name was *Slaughter*."

"Slaughter?" Kia asked. "I like where this is going."

I didn't like where it was going, where it was or where it came from.

"I first met Bart when I was in training to become a park ranger. I looked up and saw this man — big thick beard, broad shoulders, standing head and shoulders above everybody else there."

"That sounds like you," Kia said.

"Come to think of it, he does look a bit like me . . . only bigger."

"Bigger than you?" I gasped.

He nodded his head. "Bigger than me. At first I thought that was why he gave me such an uneasy feeling — I'm not used to being around people who are bigger than me — but eventually I found out there was another reason."

"Probably something to do with his name," Kia said.

"Not just his name," Dan said. He stopped and took a sip from his coffee cup. "Most of us — the rangers — were university educated and city raised. Not Bart. He was a mountain man."

"A mountain man?" Kia asked.

Dan nodded. "Born, raised and educated in the wilds. Matter of fact, on the weekends, when we had time away from our studies, most of us rangers-in-training relaxed and went to town for some fun. Bart never joined us. He grabbed his pack and headed out into the bush, living off the land and showing up again Monday morning."

"Was he doing terrible things out in the bush?" Kia asked.

Dan looked confused. "He was just living

off the land. He wasn't used to being around people and I think he just needed the time to go into the woods and clear his head."

"Well that's boring," she said.

"You have to remember, Kia, this isn't a story, this is *real*."

Kia gave me a look like "yeah, right." I had to admit that it did seem like every second scary story in the world started with something about "this really isn't a story," but Dan didn't strike me as the sort of guy who made things up.

"We all graduated and became rangers, and I lost track of Bart. He was sent to a park in one part of the country and I was sent to another park. It's a big country and there are lots of rangers. Then, seven years ago, I was transferred out here to this park . . . to replace Bart."

"Replace him?" Kia questioned. "Where did he go?"

"That's the thing," Dan said. "Nobody really knows. He lived in the ranger house — the house where we live — for almost seven years. But what seemed to happen over the years was that little by little he had less and less to do with the other rangers. It got to the point that he stopped answering the radio calls or going

70

to meetings. Finally they sent somebody out to look for him. When they got to our house, it was obvious that nobody had been living there for a long time — maybe years."

"Then where had he been living?" Kia asked.

"In the bush somewhere, in the forest. They tried to find him. They used air search, sent out rangers, even used dogs, but nobody could find him."

"He was never seen again?" I asked.

"If he'd just stayed missing it would have been mysterious enough, but he didn't. There'd be sightings of him throughout the park."

"Sightings?"

Dan shook his head. "A hiker would look up and see him moving through the trees. Campers would see a shadowy figure standing there on the outside of the halo of light thrown out by their campfire. He'd just appear and then disappear, slipping back into the bush."

I started to slowly scan the trees that surrounded us.

In the dim twilight I could see hundreds of places where somebody might be standing. And my mind couldn't help but pick out a rock or a bush that looked like a person standing or crouching down, watching us.

"And then the sightings stopped," Dan said.

I sighed in relief and the objects in the forest once again became trees and rocks and bushes.

"And that's when the actions began," Dan continued, and I felt a tingle go up my spine.

"At first it was little things. A group of campers had to come back early because they couldn't find the matches they knew they'd packed, or the propane tanks were empty — tanks they'd filled just before they went out. Maybe food that was tied up in a tree for safety just vanished. There always seemed to be something that would happen that would force those campers or hikers to come back early — to have to leave the forest. And then things got worse."

Dan paused and I held my breath.

"It was awful. Campers would wake up and find themselves looking up into the morning sky."

"What's wrong with that?" Kia asked.

"What's wrong is that they were in tents. Sometime in the middle of the night, while they were sleeping, somebody had taken a knife and cut away the entire top of the tent."

A shiver went from the tip of my toes to the top of my head.

"Or the bottom of their sleeping bag was

missing . . . the sleeping bag had been severed, cut off, only a few inches from their toes. Coleman stoves sat on the ground in pieces, packs were shredded, ropes and lines cut into lengths no longer than your hand. And nobody ever saw or heard anything."

"But they knew it was Bart," Kia said.

"They didn't know anything. They just thought. Everybody knew that Bart didn't like people being out here in the woods. He never liked tourists, campers, city folk being out here and it was like he was trying to drive them out of the park, out of *his* park."

"It would have driven me out," I admitted.

"It did most people. But not all of them," Dan said. "And that's when it got *bad . . . really* bad . . . *evil* bad." Dan paused again and then stood up. "Maybe Ned was right. I shouldn't be telling this story. Especially not here."

"Why not here?" Kia asked anxiously.

Dan didn't answer.

"Why not here?" she pressed.

"Because . . . because this is where it happened."

"Where he cut the top off the tent?" she asked.

"Where he cut the top off the *people* . . . with a chainsaw."

I gasped.

"I was the one that found them," Dan said. He started pacing around the campsite. "They'd been reported missing . . . overdue two days . . . I was sent out to try and find them and — " Dan suddenly stopped mid-sentence. He looked all around. Even in the dim light I could see the look of fear on his face.

"Do you hear it?" he asked.

"Hear what?" I croaked.

"Listen."

I turned my head. I couldn't hear anything except for the crickets and the hooting of an owl . . . and then suddenly the night exploded with the roar of an engine — a chainsaw engine!

Kia and I jumped to our feet. He was here! Bart was here with his chainsaw and he was going to — the engine noise died, replaced by the sound of Dan laughing.

"Come on out, Ned!" he yelled.

Ned walked out of the shadows. In his hands was the chainsaw. On his face was a goofy smile.

If I hadn't been so relieved, I could have killed somebody myself.

Chapter Seven

"I hope you're okay about us tricking you like that," Ned said.

"I'm okay. We're both okay," I said.

"It was just a joke."

"I know it was just a joke. I knew it last night, and I knew it this morning, and I knew it all day when you kept apologizing," I said. "It's okay, Ned. You can stop now. Honestly, it's really okay."

"It was better than okay," Kia added. "That was simply the best. When did you and your dad work all that out . . . you know, you coming out with the chainsaw?"

"Yesterday when we were hiking. We talked about it when you two were walking behind us."

I wasn't thrilled with the whole thing — actually I had been really, really close to wetting myself — but looking back it had been pretty good. The best story I'd ever heard. And last night, even when I knew it was just a joke, I still had difficulty going to sleep. When I woke up I was happy to see that our tent still had a top.

The walk back to their house was obviously the same distance the walk away from it had been. But somehow now it didn't seem as bad. Maybe it was because I already knew how far we had to travel, or maybe because I was thinking that once we got back I could sleep indoors in a bed.

As far as camping was concerned, I took after my father. He said his idea of camping involved a soft bed, cable TV and a good restaurant where he could get breakfast in the morning.

"Do you know where we are?" Kia asked Ned.

"I have a rough idea."

"So if we were separated from your father, could you get us back to your house?"

"I could . . . I'm pretty sure I could."

That wasn't really too reassuring. Somehow it now seemed even more important to keep Dan in sight.

"This was a long trip for nothing," Kia said.

"I don't understand," Ned said.

"You know, we walked all this way to look

for some people who weren't there anyway," she explained.

"But we got to go for a hike and go camping," Ned said. "That's always good."

"I don't know about always, but it was good this time," Kia said.

We moved along through the forest. Dan was out in front, scouting a path, and Ned, Kia and I followed behind in single file. The mid-day sun had passed and it was already cooler — or at least not as hot. I couldn't help thinking how different this was than taking a walk in my neighborhood — how different life was for Ned. This was okay for a vacation, but I couldn't imagine living like this, away from everything and everybody. I liked my parents, but I wouldn't want them to be my only company 24/7. It was just so strange to be so far away from other people all the time.

"Look, there's a road!" Kia called out.

I hurried to catch up to where she and Ned stood. A long brown ribbon cut through the forest.

"That's the road that leads to our house. It's in that direction," Ned said, pointing off to the left.

"So are we going to walk the rest of the way along the road?" I asked.

"I guess so. It's not far now," he said.

"Not far like a couple of minutes or not far like a couple of hours?" I questioned.

"Maybe thirty minutes," Ned said.

"Maybe we won't have to walk. Why don't we stick out our thumbs and try to hitch a ride with somebody?" Kia suggested and then laughed at her own joke.

"After walking through the forest, up and down hills and around rocks and ponds, walking on a road is practically going to feel like a drive," I said.

We scrambled down the rise and to the road. Dan was waiting there for us, crouching on the ground, studying the dirt.

"Tracks," he said. "Fairly new . . . more than one set."

"There's been traffic along here?" I asked.

"More than usual. Somebody has been driving along this trail."

"But our house is the only place farther down the road than here, and with the restrictions on park entry who could it be?" Ned asked.

Almost in answer there came the sound of an engine. My instant, anxious response was that it was a chainsaw motor — Bart's chainsaw. But then a truck appeared around the curve . . . it looked like Ned's truck.

"It's Mom!" Ned yelled out.

Fantastic! We weren't going to have to walk any farther.

"She's moving awfully fast," Ned said.

"As far as I'm concerned she's always moving too fast," Dan said.

The truck came racing along the trail, and the horn started to blare out. She skidded to a stop and a cloud of dust rolled over top of us. She jumped out of the truck.

"I'm so glad I found you!" Debbie yelled. "I thought you'd come back this way, so I've been up and down this road half a dozen times."

That explained the tracks, but not why she was so glad to find us so quickly.

"Everybody get into the truck and I'll explain."

Debbie jumped back behind the wheel and we tossed in our packs and climbed into the truck. She started driving — driving away from their house.

"You were going to explain," Dan said.

"The radio call came in last night," Debbie said. "There's a fire southeast of the park."

"How big?" Dan asked.

"Big enough that they're pulling most of

the park rangers, including you, to fight it. The team is assembling in Salmon Arm."

"How soon?" Dan asked, looking at his watch.

"Pretty well right now. That's why I was trying to intercept you on the road. I've got all your gear in the back of the truck."

"Then we better move it."

Kia turned to Ned, sitting beside her. "How far away is this Salmon place?" she whispered.

"Salmon Arm," he said, "is about three hours from here."

"Not the way I'm going to be driving today," Debbie said. "Sorry you all have to come along but there's no choice. Dan can't drive himself because then we'd be left without a vehicle, and I can't leave the three of you alone."

"That's okay," Kia said.

"Besides, it'll give me a chance to do some grocery shopping, and the two city kids might be wanting a little taste of civilization by now anyway."

Landing at Kelowna had been nothing compared to the bumps and bounces of the first part of the ride. The only smooth parts were when we were actually catching air between the bumps as Debbie rocketed along the road. Hitting the highway the ride was smoother but the speed was faster. I mentioned something about being afraid of getting a speeding ticket, but Dan said no policeman will ever ticket somebody on the way to fight a fire.

We slowed down as we started passing houses and businesses and drive-through restaurants along the highway. The road sliced between high, high hills — not quite mountains but bigger than anything I'd ever want to climb or slide down on a toboggan. The hills were marked by jutting rocks, steep sides and a sparse growth of small, stunted trees.

"Welcome to Salmon Arm," Debbie said.

"I didn't even know salmon had arms," Kia replied.

"Or legs for that matter," Dan said, "but that's not how it got its name."

"The town sits on the banks of Shuswap Lake. It has five different parts, or arms, and this one had more salmon in it, so this is the Salmon Arm of the lake," Ned explained.

Debbie slowed the truck down even more as we started to meet traffic and then came to a complete stop at a red light. I looked around. The highway was lined with hotels and stores and places to eat. There was a movie theater — it was even a multiplex — and there was a mall . . . a real genuine mall! The light changed and we started moving again.

"This place looks pretty big," I said. "How many people live here?"

"The population swells in the summer," Dan said, "but year-round it's about fifteen thousand people."

"Possibly soon to be fifteen thousand and three," Debbie said.

"Is this where you might be moving to?" I asked.

"This is the place. We'd be living just outside of town. Ned would be going to school here."

I looked over at Ned. I was wondering how he was feeling about all of this. If it was me, I'd be pretty nervous about going to a new school — especially if I'd never gone to *any* school before.

I'd gone to the same school my whole life, but I'd seen enough new kids start to know that it wasn't always easy — especially if you were a little different. Ned was a nice guy, but he was a lot more than a little different.

I wished he was going to be coming to my school where Kia and I could take care of him.

"Is it just me or does anybody else smell smoke?" Kia asked.

"That's from the forest fire," Dan said.

"Is it that close?" she exclaimed.

"Over one hundred kilometers away."

"And we can smell it here?"

"The smoke from a big fire can travel thousands of kilometers," Dan explained.

While that sounded hard to believe, I knew that Dan knew what he was talking about.

"And the smoke tends to roll into the valleys. That's why you can smell it here," Debbie added.

"Sometimes it's more than just the smoke that rolls into the valleys," Dan said. "Sometimes it's the fire."

"There's been a fire here?" I asked.

"It came along the valley, burned up a whole lot of timber, homes, some businesses," Dan said. "The highway was closed and the whole town had to be evacuated."

"Did you notice how the hills just back there on our left looked pretty bare?" Debbie asked.

"I noticed that," I said.

"The fire got that far, right to the edge of the town. The whole place would have burned up if it wasn't for the work of the firefighters."

"That and a change in the weather and wind direction," Dan said. "It was close."

Debbie pulled the truck into a mall. There, in the middle of the parking lot, away from the building, sat a couple of big buses surrounded by cars. She pulled into an empty spot. There were lots of people milling around as we got out of the truck.

"Looks like we made it in time," Debbie said.

Dan circled around to the back of the truck and reached in for a gigantic backpack. There were tools hanging down — a big axe and a shovel. As he pulled it out and swung it onto his shoulders a basketball bounced out of the back of the truck and started to roll away.

"I got it!" I yelled out as I scrambled after it. I grabbed the ball and dribbled it back, setting it down in the truck.

"In case I'm not back before you have to fly home, I hope you kids enjoy the rest of your visit," Dan said.

"You mean you might be gone that long?" Kia asked.

"Could be a few days or it could be a few

weeks. Depends on the fire and the weather and I have no control over either of those things," Dan explained.

We all walked around to the front of the truck.

"Ned," Dan said, "I want you to help out your mother in any way you can and look after your animals and your friends . . . okay?"

Ned nodded his head but didn't answer. Dan wrapped an arm around Ned and Ned hugged him back. Debbie came over and joined in, making a family hug.

"Be careful," Debbie said, "and don't go being any hero."

"Yes, Mother," he scoffed.

"I don't care what you think, you just be careful! You're big, but you're not as big as a fire!"

He nodded his head. "I'll be careful . . . I promise. Now I better get going."

Dan tried to walk away but both Ned and Debbie held on a little bit longer. Debbie gave him a kiss and then released him. Dan walked across the parking lot and joined up with a group of men already dressed in big boots and wearing helmets.

"He'll be okay," Debbie said quietly to Ned.

Ned nodded his head ever so slightly. He looked like he was going to cry . . . What was the problem? He was only going to be gone for a few days or a couple of weeks at most and . . . then I noticed the tears running down Debbie's cheeks.

"Is this . . . is this dangerous?" I asked.

"Fighting forest fires is always dangerous," Debbie said as she took the back of her hand and brushed away the tears. "But Dan is trained — all of them are trained — so they know what they're doing and how to do it safely. He'll be fine."

I nodded my head. I wondered if she'd been just answering my question or trying to convince both Ned and herself that everything would be alright.

All of the firefighters — mostly men, but a few women as well — climbed up into the big buses. As the last person got in, the door closed and the bus started away. The people remaining in the parking lots waved and yelled out last minute good-byes, and I noticed that it wasn't just Debbie who was in tears. We stood there and waved until the buses circled the parking lot, took one of the exits onto the highway and then got smaller and smaller until they disappeared around the curve in the highway.

People still stood in small groups and talked. Some started filtering back to their cars or trucks and began to leave.

"I guess there's no point in us staying here any longer," Debbie said. "I've got some grocery shopping to do."

"Do we have to go shopping?" Ned asked.

"Well if there's something else — "

"How about some basketball?" I asked, remembering the ball. "There's got to be a court around here somewhere, isn't there?"

"Just behind the mall," Ned said. "We can walk there."

"Then what are we waiting for?" Kia asked.

Chapter Eight

We walked along the street, dribbling and passing the ball back and forth. There were big and little houses, nice lawns and large flower gardens. This certainly wasn't exactly like the city where we lived, but it was a lot closer to what we were used to. I didn't think there was any way I could live way out in the bush where Ned lived, but this would be okay. Not that I wanted to ever move anywhere, but this looked like a nice place. We came up to a school.

"The courts are in the back," Ned said. "This is the school I'd be going to if we moved."

"Looks nice," I said.

"It's just a bunch of bricks and books . . . you know, your typical school," Kia said.

I heard voices yelling out and the unmistakable sound of a basketball bouncing against the pavement. I loved that sound. We hurried around the side and came to the schoolyard. There were two basketball courts and there was a game happening on one of them — older kids . . . teenagers.

As we walked over I watched the game in progress. The kids looked to be at least four or five years older than us. They weren't bad, but it was obvious they were just street ball players — lots of long shots, no plays, not many passes and nobody seemed to be interested in defense.

"Want to watch or play?" Ned asked.

"Play," Kia answered. "Nothing that anybody here is going to do is worth watching."

That sounded awfully arrogant, but I had to agree. We played rep ball, in the city, with some of the best players in the whole country. What were some guys on a court behind some school in a place called *Salmon Arm* going to show us about basketball?

"They look pretty good," Ned said as he watched the action.

"That's only because you've been playing against your mother most of the time," I snapped and then instantly regretted my words.

"I guess you're right . . . although she is pretty good."

We walked onto the empty court. Both ends of the court looked fine. There were solid backboards, the rims were straight and they even had mesh. That was something you didn't see very often where we lived. Usually playground nets had tattered or missing mesh and the rims were bent down from people hanging on them. I guess people were more respectful out here. Or maybe they just couldn't get enough air to hang.

"What do you want to play?" Kia asked.

"Bump would be great . . . if we had another ball," I said. "How about horse?"

"Works for me," Kia replied.

"What's horse?" Ned asked.

"It's a simple game. We take turns taking a shot."

"Difficult shots," Kia added.

"Yeah, the harder the better. A shot you can make but you don't think the other two can make."

"And if you make the shot and they miss it, then they get a letter on them," Kia continued.

"A letter?"

"Like an 'h' or 'o' or whatever," I explained.

"And when you get all the letters on you that spell horse, then you're out. Does that make sense?"

"I guess so," Ned said. "I just wish I had some trick shots."

"Just shoot from far away or make it a bank shot off the rim or even a hook shot," Kia suggested. "The way you were making those three-point shots back at your place means that would be a good shot for you to try."

"Let's play," I said.

It didn't take long before Ned had been "lettered" out and was sitting watching Kia and me finish the game. Actually, though, he was spending just as much time staring at the school. I figured I knew what he was thinking about.

"We have an audience," Kia said.

I looked behind me. There were three guys — they looked around our age — standing at the edge of the court. One of them was holding a basketball.

"How about if we put on a little show?" Kia asked.

"How about if we finish the game?"

"Me putting on a show should finish the game," she said. "You're only an 'e' short of losing."

"Last time I checked you were only missing one letter too," I argued.

"That's just going to make it more heartbreaking for you. Getting *so* close and then losing."

I shook my head. "You taunting me only makes the win sweeter. Your shot," I said and stuffed the ball into her hands.

Kia walked well past the three-point line. I knew exactly what she was going to do. Kia loved the long shot, the last-minute buzzer-beater. When we were playing for real in a game, I knew she was the one who always tried to get the ball into her hands to take that last, long shot. If she made it, she was a hero. If she missed, who could blame her?

Kia set up. The odds were against her making this, but she was a pretty good outside shooter — certainly better than I was. She lined up the shot and put it up. High, clean shot aiming right for the hoop and — it clanked off the rim and bounced harmlessly away. I scrambled after the ball.

"Now it's my turn," I said.

"No problem. I can make any shot that you can — you're not going to do that bounce shot are you?" she demanded.

"I wasn't going to — that is until you mentioned it."

"Don't. It's a stupid shot!"

"You only think it's stupid because you can't do it."

"I'd think it was stupid if I was the only one in the world who could do it. Stupid is stupid! Just don't do it!"

I smiled. "If you want me to stop using the shot, then you're going to have to learn to do it yourself."

I walked to the foul line and held the ball like I was going to take a regular shot. I then bounced the ball on the ground so that it gracefully angled up and dropped right into the net!

"Now it's your turn," I said.

She took the ball. "You win."

"Aren't you even going to try?" I asked.

"I'd rather lose than look stupid."

"Then how about if we play some real basketball?"

"What did you have in mind?" Kia asked.

"Let's see if those kids want to play," I suggested, gesturing to the three kids who were now shooting at the hoop at the other end.

"You want to play with them?" she asked.

"Why not? They look about our age. We

could have a game of three-on-three. Us against them."

"That wouldn't be basketball, that would be a massacre," Kia said.

"Who knows . . . maybe they're good."

"Yeah, right, when I think of good basketball players I always think of Salmon Arm," she said and laughed.

"But that's why I want to play them."

"Because we can kill them?" Kia asked.

"No, because they *are* from around here. Maybe they even go to this school . . . the school that Ned is maybe going to be going to in the fall."

"So he can meet some of the kids," she said.

"Exactly. And so they can see that he can play ball and has cool friends who can play ball. Does that make sense?"

"Perfect," she agreed. "Tell you what, you get Ned and I'll go and talk to them."

Kia strolled toward the kids and I went over to talk to Ned. He was sitting in the shade, his back against a tree, staring off into space. I didn't know if he was thinking about the school or what was happening with his father, but it was clear he wasn't here.

"Ned, come on, we're going to play a game."

"A game?"

"Yeah, me, you and Kia against those guys," I said, pointing to where Kia was talking to them. "It will be like the Salmon Arm version of a three-on-three contest."

Ned slowly unfolded his legs and got to his feet. We got to the center of the court just as Kia and the three boys got there.

"This is Tom and Jeff and . . . "

"Frank," the third boy said.

"Yeah, Frank. This is Ned and Nick," she said.

Everybody mumbled greetings and nodded their head.

"So since there's six of us, how about a little game of three-on-three?" Kia asked.

"I guess that would be okay," one of the boys — I didn't know if he was Tom or Jeff — said.

"But what are the teams going to be?" asked the other.

"We were thinking the three of us against the three of you," I said.

"I don't know," he said, shaking his head. "I don't think that would be much of a game . . . we're pretty good."

What did he mean, *we're pretty good*? I glanced over at Kia. She looked as stunned as I felt.

"You know we can play basketball," I said.

"We're talking about a real game, right?" one of them asked. "Not trick shots like that bouncing thing?"

"That's not a trick shot," Kia said. "That's a *stupid* shot."

All three of the boys started to laugh. "We were thinking the same thing," one of them said.

"Let's just play some ball," I snapped angrily. "And since you three are so great, how about we get the ball first?"

"Sure, why not?" one of them asked.

"But are these teams going to be fair?" asked Tom.

"It doesn't matter. It's just a game. They have the big guy so it might be okay," Frank said. He turned to Ned. "You play much ball?"

"Just by myself at my house."

"We'll even use your ball," I said as I took it from Frank's hands. I walked away and Kia and Ned trailed behind me.

"I was going to say let's take it easy on

them," I said. "Now let's just *kill* them. Show them how basketball is played in the city."

"But I'm not from any city," Ned said.

"Then play like you did when you were in the city."

I turned to face them. They were lined up ready for us. "Rebounds of the other team's shots or steals have to be taken outside the three-point line," I said.

"That's how we usually play," Frank said. "How about baskets are worth a single point and anything outside the three is worth two points?"

"That works for us. Check." I tossed the ball to one of them and he tossed it back.

"Monarch!" I screamed. That was one of the plays we'd used to win the Hoop Crazy tournament in Toronto the summer before.

Ned went to the top of the key and Kia used him for the screen. I put the ball in to her and she almost instantly tossed it back to me. Ned broke from the high post to the low position and I lobbed in a pass, well above the head of the man covering him. Effortlessly Ned tossed the ball up and it dropped!

"Is that tricky enough for you?" I asked as one of them took the ball and walked it back to the top of the key.

"Cool it," Kia hissed in my ear. "We'd like these kids to like Ned, remember? So take it easy."

"Yeah . . . fine . . . okay," I muttered. I'd take it easy as soon as we were up by ten baskets and there was no doubt in anybody's mind who could and could not play ball.

They checked the ball. I was going out on my man when he threw up a long three-point shot . . . It dropped!

"That's *my* idea of a trick shot," the player said. "That's two to one for us."

Kia picked up the loose ball and walked over to me. "So much for being nice. Now let's go back to the killing 'em part."

"That's game!" I yelled as Ned's shot dropped through the net. Ned and Kia and I exchanged a high five.

"Good game," Frank said. He walked over and, to my complete surprise, shook my hand, then Kia's and Ned's. The other two did the same thing.

"You guys can play," one of the others said.

"Guys and *girl*," Kia corrected him.

"It was a close game," I commented. Actually a lot closer than I would have expected.

Winning fifteen points to eleven wasn't exactly the beating I'd imagined.

"We just thought we'd win," Frank said. "We play on the Salmon Arm travel team."

"A travel team?" I asked.

"We travel all around the province and represent Salmon Arm in tournaments against other places."

"Where we come from we call it a rep team because you represent your city, or, I guess, town. Do you play against all the other towns in the area?" I asked.

"All the other places in the whole province. We came in fourth last year," Frank said.

"That's pretty good," Kia said. "We play rep too. Our team finished *second* last year." Kia paused.

"We took first the year before that," Frank said. "Salmon Arm is famous for having some of the best teams in the province. Especially our girls' teams."

"I didn't know that," Kia said. "We're not from around here."

"We figured that," one of them scoffed. "We know everybody in town and we didn't know you."

"So you three all live right in town?" I asked.

"You can see all of our houses from here."

"And do you go to this school?" Kia asked.

"Yep. All of us are in grade five."

"That's a coincidence," I said. "We're in grade five too."

"And a bigger coincidence is that Ned is probably even going to be going to this school next year," Kia said, pointing at the building.

"Not this one," one of them said.

"Yeah, this one," Ned said.

"Can't be. This school only goes to grade six."

"I'm only going into grade five," Ned said.

All three of them looked shocked, as if they didn't believe what he had just said.

"Did you fail or something?" Frank asked.

"Or fail a couple of times?" asked one of the others.

"No," Ned said, shaking his head.

"How old are you?"

"I turned ten in April," Ned replied.

"April 23," I added. "I'm three hours older than Ned."

"You're joking . . . right?" Frank asked.

"No. I'm ten."

"And you're moving here . . . to Salmon Arm?"

"It's not definite, but my parents think so. We'd be moving in so I could start school in the fall."

"And when you move, you're going to want to play basketball, right?" Frank questioned.

"I'd like to . . . do you think I could play with you guys?"

Frank started laughing. "Look, give me your phone number and I'll call Coach and — "

"We don't have a phone," Ned said, cutting him off.

"You don't have a phone? Everybody in the whole world has a phone!"

"Not us. We live pretty far up in the mountains so — "

"Look, I'll give you *my* phone number and as soon as you know you're moving here, you call me. We'll come over that day and help you move in!"

"Gee, thanks, that's nice of you," Ned gushed.

Frank turned to Kia and me. "Do you know why we finished fourth instead of first last year?"

"Why?" Kia asked.

"No height." Frank turned back to Ned. "You move in here and we'll make sure you have a whole team of kids who'll be your friends."

"Gee, that sounds great!" Ned said.

Just then there was a honking sound. I turned around. Debbie had pulled into the parking lot.

"It looks like we have to get going," Ned said.

"Not until I give you my number . . . and remember, you call, okay?"

Ned nodded his head. "I'll call."

"Promise?"

"I promise."

"Here, let me get some paper and a pen and I'll write it down."

"My mother will have those in the car. Come on and I'll introduce you three to my mother."

Kia bent down and picked up our basketball. "I'd say that went a little bit better than okay."

"That went really well."

"You know the only way it could have been better?" she asked.

"How?"

"If we'd beaten them by more."

Chapter Nine

I woke up with a start. What was that sound? I listened to the rhythmic patter . . . It was rain! I sat up in my bed. There was enough light flowing in through the window for me to see, so I knew it must be morning. I looked around the room. Kia was asleep on a mattress on the floor beside me, and Ned was sitting up in his bed across the room.

"Good morning," Ned whispered.

"Good morning."

"Did the storm wake you up too?" he asked.

"I guess so. What time is it?"

"Just after five-thirty," he said, pointing to the clock on his dresser glowing out the time.

"This rain is good news," I said. "Especially for your dad and the other guys fighting the fire."

"I doubt it's even raining where they are. Storms in the mountains are usually pretty local and stay in one of the valleys. Especially storms like this."

"Like what?"

In answer there was an explosion of thunder and I practically jumped to my feet.

"That was close," I croaked.

"Really close and that's what's got me worried," Ned said.

I wanted to chuckle but then thought better of it. His father had been hit by lightning so I guess he had reason to be scared.

"I used to be afraid of lightning when I was little, but there's really nothing to be worried about when you're in a house. You're perfectly safe."

"That isn't what I'm worried about," Ned answered. "You know how most forest fires are caused by humans?"

"Yeah?"

"Well lightning strikes are the second biggest cause. And it's most dangerous when there are drought conditions and everything is dry."

"But it's not dry now, it's raining," I argued. The gentle patter had given way to a pounding on the roof. It was really coming down.

"It was a really big storm, but a sudden downpour like this just runs off because the ground is baked hard. It floods the streams but doesn't really wet the ground enough to make a difference."

"Maybe we should just go back to sleep," I suggested.

"I wasn't sleeping anyway. I was thinking about how different things are going to be for me if we move."

"Different isn't bad sometimes," I said.

"I guess not."

The house practically shook as the sound of thunder roared and then echoed off to silence, leaving only the sound of the rain.

"Thanks for what you did," Ned said.

"What?"

"Getting those guys to play. I know you did that for me."

"I did that so we could play some basketball!" I protested.

"No you didn't," Ned said. "And it's going to make things easier for me now." He paused. "I know I'm different than most people."

"But remember that different isn't bad."

"Sometimes. Sometimes it is. I know when kids are making fun of me," Ned said.

"Only a jerk would do that."

"You used to make fun of me," Ned said.

"That's because I used to be a jerk," I said and Ned started to laugh.

"Just be yourself," I added. "And it doesn't hurt that you can play ball. Didn't you see how excited those kids were about having you on their team?"

"That's just because I'm big."

"Big is something you can't coach. Every team needs height. Besides, you are getting better . . . a lot better," I argued.

"Thanks."

"And one more thing. Because you are so much bigger than everybody else, if somebody really, really gives you a hard time, then threaten to pound 'em."

"You want me to hit them?"

"Not hit them. Just *threaten* to hit them. Stand over top of them and say something like, 'Do you really want to get me mad at you?'"

"But won't that get me in trouble?" Ned asked.

"Probably not nearly as much trouble as not threatening them might cause."

I turned my head and listened. Not only was there no more thunder, but I didn't even hear the rain or the wind anymore.

"It's stopped," I said.

Ned climbed out of bed. "I better have a look around."

I jumped out of bed and trailed after Ned. Kia was still sound asleep. That girl could sleep through anything. Walking into the living room I saw Debbie already there, standing by the window, looking out.

"Morning, boys. Did the storm wake you up too?" she asked.

"Bad storm," Ned said. "Do you see anything?"

"Nothing. I was just waiting for one of you to get up and then I was going to go out and look around," she said.

"How about if we go out?" Ned asked.

"That would be fine. Don't go too far though, and I'll have breakfast waiting when you get back."

Ned and I quickly got into our clothes. He put on his hiking boots and I did up my basketball shoes.

Stepping outside I was amazed at how much cooler it had become. The air felt cold and moist as I inhaled a big breath. We started walking up the road. It was littered with leaves and branches — small and large — which had been knocked down by the wind and rain. The winds were still very strong. I stopped and bent down to pick up a bigger branch that I could use as a walking stick. I snapped off the top, breaking it over my knee.

"Do you smell that?" Ned asked.

"What?" I demanded. He didn't answer. I took a deep breath and . . . smoke.

"Do you smell it?" he asked again.

"I don't smell anything," I said, although I did smell something . . . it was like burning toast.

"You can't smell smoke?" Ned asked.

I took a deep breath. "I guess I can, but maybe it's from the fire that your father is fighting and the storm winds just blew it here."

"The storm blew in from the other direction."

Ned bent down and picked up a handful of pine needles. He let them go and they were caught up in the wind and scattered.

"Whatever is causing the smoke is in that direction," he said, pointing up the road.

I anxiously scanned the horizon. I couldn't see any smoke or fire. I couldn't see anything except trees and rocks and the mountains in the background.

"Come on," Ned said as he started up the road.

"Shouldn't we go back and tell your mother?"

"Tell her what? That we thought we smelled smoke but we didn't see any fire or smoke rising up but we think there might just be a fire out there, somewhere?"

I stayed right by Ned's side. "What do we do if there's a fire?"

"If it's small — really small — we put it out."

"You know how to do that?"

"I've read all about it, remember?"

"And if it's not a small fire?" I asked.

"Then we tell my mother and she radios in the location and we get out of here and *fast*."

I liked the idea of getting away, but I didn't like the way he said "fast."

"When you said fast, how fast did you mean?" I asked.

"Really fast. A forest fire can move with more speed than a person can run."

I gulped. "You've seen that?"

He shook his head. "Of course not, but I've read about it. The fire jumps from tree-top to treetop and the tops of the trees just sort of explode. It's supposed to sound like a cannon going off."

"If it can move that fast, should we be heading up to look for it?" I asked.

"There isn't much of a wind to drive it. Besides, we don't have any choice."

Of course we had a choice. We could just turn around and get out of here.

Ned left the road and headed along a trail that went almost straight up one of the hills. I figured he was going to higher ground to scout the area. I kept scanning the sky in all directions, looking for telltale signs of smoke that would show the location of a fire. I didn't see anything, but between the rocks, trees and hills there really wasn't that much that I could see.

"There it is," Ned said and I bumped into him from behind.

I looked up to where Ned was pointing. There was a thick plume of smoke rising up from the ground. As it cleared the tops of the trees the strong winds blew it away so the smoke couldn't be seen from a distance.

"Is it big?" I asked anxiously.

"Too big for me to fight. We have to get back." Ned turned and started running back down the trail. I sprinted after him. He was ahead of me as we reached the road. I was running as fast as I could, but he was pulling farther ahead on those long legs of his.

"Wait up!" I yelled. I didn't want to be left behind.

"Every minute counts now," Ned yelled back over his shoulder.

I doubled my efforts and started to close the gap between us. Little by little I got closer, although it felt like my lungs were going to burst. The smell of the smoke became stronger in my nose. That didn't make sense — we were leaving the flames behind. Maybe it was because I was sucking so much air into my lungs to keep up with Ned.

The house came into sight and I stopped running. I wasn't going to catch him anyway, and I was safe here. Ned continued to run. As I walked I looked back over my shoulder as if I was afraid the fire was going to suddenly burst into the open and be right behind me. I didn't see anything. There was no smoke in the sky, no flames, just trees. If I hadn't seen it with my own eyes — if I wasn't still smelling it in my nose — I wouldn't have believed it.

The door to the house was open. As I walked in, Debbie was already on the shortwave radio calling in the report.

"Yep, we have a burn," she said into the microphone. "Lightning strike, less than a kilometer from our location. Do you copy?"

"Copy," came a static-filled voice. "Can it be controlled?"

"Not here. We need support."

"That's a problem," the voice responded. "There's no support in the area. Soonest ETA is six hours at best."

"ETA?" I asked Ned.

"Estimated time of arrival," he explained.

"Lots of fuel to feed this fire," Debbie said. "Six hours isn't good enough. Any chance of sooner?"

"It's as good as we can get. All firefighters are already out on assignment battling other blazes."

"I copy," Debbie said. "I have three children with me so I'm going to evacuate my position."

"Seems wise. Get out as soon as possible."

"Will do. Roger and out."

She put down the microphone and looked over at us. "I think somebody better get Kia up."

Chapter Ten

"I don't know what the rush is about," Kia said.

There were now pillars of smoke visible along the horizon.

"It's growing and growing fast," I said. "You can see it and smell it."

"I smell it more than I did a while ago, but the smell of smoke isn't going to kill anybody."

"It's not the smell I'm worried about." I couldn't help thinking about what Ned had told me about how fast a fire could move if there were strong winds. I could just picture the fire moving from tree to tree, coming down the valley right to where we were standing.

"Just hurry," I said as I put my pack into the back of the truck. Already in the back were three little cages holding Ned's pets.

"These are heavy," Kia said. "Hold the door for me."

I held it open and she put down the load she was carrying — picture albums. Debbie was packing the truck up with all sorts of personal things because she was afraid that the fire would spread to their house.

Debbie came out of the house. She was carrying the shortwave radio. She said it was worth thousands of dollars. I ran over and opened the passenger door and she carefully placed the large shortwave radio set on the seat.

"What more do we still have to get?" I asked.

"There's lots of things we could bring, but that's all we have time to take. We have to get going."

"So we're going to get going now?" I said. The sooner we left the better.

"As soon as Ned is finished."

Ned had hooked up a pump and hose to their well and was spraying the ground around the house with water, soaking it down, so if the fire did spread this way it might stop before reaching the house. Ned dropped the hose to the ground and the water continued to flow out onto the ground.

"I don't know how much more water is left in the well, but it's better to be up here than down there."

"That's a smart idea," Debbie said. "Now everybody in. It's time to go."

I climbed into the back seat and Ned and Kia climbed in beside me.

"Do you think the house will be okay?" Ned asked.

"I'm sure it will be." Debbie turned around to face us. "I hope it will be. There's nothing more we can do. Maybe the response team will be here sooner than they said."

She started driving. Ned looked out the window at their house, turning his head to keep looking at it as we moved up the trail.

"It'll be okay," I said. "Either way it's going to be okay."

Ned nodded his head.

"Is it just me or does it smell like we're getting closer to the fire?" Kia asked.

"The winds swirl around in the hills," Ned said.

I could smell the smoke . . . but I could also see it. The road up ahead looked a little bit like there was mist or fog.

"Mom . . . do you see — "

"I see it," she said, cutting him off. She looked back over her shoulder at us. "There's nothing to be worried — "

"Look out!" I screamed as the road in front of us was blocked.

Debbie cranked the wheel of the truck and slammed on the brakes. We skidded sideways. Suddenly everything seemed to be happening in slow motion — like the video replay in a basketball game. Kia screamed . . . the seat belt tightened across my chest . . . Ned was yelling too. . . my hands came up to brace myself against the seat . . . and then we slid off the road and down a bank. Branches scratched at the doors and windows. Finally, with a loud thud, we slammed into a tree. Things that had been piled loosely in the back of the truck came shooting past my head. Outside, clouds of dust rose all around us. Then everything was silent.

I stared out the windshield into nothing but branches and a spiderweb of cracks running across the whole width of the glass. I wanted to call out, but I was too stunned to talk — so stunned that it was like I'd even forgotten to breathe. I took a deep breath.

"Is everybody okay?" Debbie asked, breaking the trance.

"I'm okay," Ned said.

"Me too," Kia said.

It was good to know that nobody was hurt.

"Nick?"

"Yeah?"

"Are you alright?" Debbie asked.

"Sure, I'm fine."

"How about you, Mom, are you okay?" Ned asked.

"I'm okay . . . I jammed my leg into the dashboard, but I'm okay. Everybody get out of the truck," Debbie said. "And get out carefully."

That was a good idea. I'd seen enough TV shows to know that cars that crashed often burst into flames . . . and I could smell something burning! I felt a rush of panic surge through my body and then realized that of course I smelled something burning because the forest was on fire . . . For a few fleeting seconds I'd forgotten that!

I tried my door and it hit against something with a thud, opening only a few inches. I pushed harder but it wouldn't give. I looked out the window. There were branches pinning it in place. Ned and Kia had already gotten out their door and I scrambled across the seat, moving around the things that had been thrown forward from the back, and climbed out. It felt good to be out.

The truck had left the road and gone down

a hill, plowing out a path in the trees and bush. I scrambled up the incline. Debbie had just gotten out and was standing beside the door, leaning against the truck.

"Wow, what happened?" Kia asked. I turned around. The road was blocked with trees and rocks and mud. It was like somebody had stolen the road.

"Landslide," Ned said. "The rain last night must have caused a landslide."

"But how does the truck get by it?" I asked.

"The truck doesn't. This happens sometimes. They have to send in a bulldozer to clear the way."

"Then how do we get out? How do we get away from the fire?" I asked anxiously.

"We haven't got much choice. We have to walk out."

"But it's a long way!" Kia protested.

"The highway isn't that much farther than what we walked yesterday. And as we walk out we'll probably meet the firefighting crew coming in to take care of the blaze."

"But how will *they* get through the landslide?" I asked.

"Every crew will have heavy earthmoving equipment," Ned said.

"Have what?" I asked.

"A bulldozer. They almost always . . . maybe I better radio in to let them know they need one," Ned said. "You two could go and see how far the slide goes and if it looks okay on the other side and I'll get my mother to call in our situation."

Ned started back down for the truck, and Kia walked up to where the road met the slide. I went after her. She was already climbing up and over the rocks that blocked the way.

"Be careful," I said.

"Yes, Mother," she said.

I scrambled over the rocks and caught up to her. She was standing on a boulder that had to be half the size of the truck.

"This goes on for a long way," she said.

I could see what she meant. The whole section of the road was gone. The whole hill on one side had just shifted over and it was like the road had never been there in the first place. I shuddered at the thought of what would have happened if the slide had taken place while we were on that section of the road.

"Even if we could get the truck out of the ditch there's no way it could ever get by this . . . oh, my goodness," Kia gasped.

"What is it?" I exclaimed.

She pointed at the landslide.

"I know it's big, but we can walk around it and — "

Then I saw it too. Up ahead, rising over the hills, there was smoke. There wasn't just a forest fire behind us in the valley. There was something burning in front of us! We were trapped!

Chapter Eleven

"Ned! Debbie!" I screamed as we ran toward the truck.

Debbie was slumped down on the ground, leaning against the back tire of the truck. Ned was inside the truck.

"There's a fire!" Kia yelled as we skidded to a stop.

"She means another fire!" I exclaimed.

Debbie struggled to her feet — what was wrong . . . was she hurt?

"Where's the fire?" she demanded.

"Down the valley, on the other side of the landslide!" I answered.

She hobbled to the still open driver's side door and leaned in. I rushed to her side. Ned was on the radio.

"Do you copy?" he yelled into the microphone. "Do you copy?"

There was nothing in reply but static.

"It's broken!" he said. He looked and

sounded panicky. "When we crashed it hit against the dashboard . . . I sent out the message . . . but I can't get an answer . . . Maybe they heard me!"

"Hand me the microphone," Debbie said calmly. She sounded completely opposite to the way Ned sounded — to the way I felt.

"This is Debbie. I'm broadcasting from a position approximately two kilometers south of Ranger Station 27. I don't know if you can hear. There's a fire of unknown size to the north of our position and another to the south. My truck isn't an option for transport . . . and I'm injured . . . I think my knee is either dislocated or broken."

"Broken?" I said softly to myself.

"I don't know if you can hear us . . . I don't know . . . our radio is not receiving in-coming messages . . . I just hope you can hear us. We are in need of help . . . desperate need. Over and out."

Debbie put down the microphone and then she slumped over in the seat.

"Mom, are you alright?" Ned asked.

"I'm okay," she groaned. "My leg is hurting really bad, but I'm okay."

"What do we do now?" Ned asked. "Should we go back to the house?"

"There's no point, and even if there was I couldn't get back there on this leg."

"Then what do we do?"

"I need you and Nick and Kia to go up to Summit Rock. Look all around and see the extent of the fire, I mean the fires. You need to see if there's a way out through the next valley."

"Sure, we'll go right up and have a look and — " Ned stopped. "But even if we can get out, can you make it up that slope on your leg?"

She shook her head. "I don't think so."

"So what good would it do even if we could get out that way?" Ned asked.

"It would mean that you could lead Nick and Kia through that valley and along the trails until you hit the highway."

We could do that. It was a long walk, but as long as we were moving away from the fire I'd be alright with that.

"And what about you?"

That was right, what about Debbie? There was no way she could make that climb. She could hardly walk.

"I'd wait here until the fire crew arrives," she said.

"You want us to just leave you here?" Kia asked in disbelief.

"I'll be just fine."

"I'm not leaving you here!" Ned snapped.

"You have to. Kia and Nick could never find their way to the highway without your help."

"I'm not leaving you!" Ned protested again. "You're hurt."

"I'm not hurt that badly. It's just my leg."

"We're not just walking away," Ned said.

"I'll be fine here . . . I'll just wait right here until help arrives."

Ned nodded his head. "You're saying you'll be fine if you stay here . . . right?"

"Of course I will," she said reassuringly.

"In that case it's settled," Ned said.

"You mean we're leaving your mother here?" I asked. That just didn't sound right.

"No. It's settled that I'm not leaving. I'll wait right here for them too."

"No, you're not!" Debbie protested. "Kia and Nick need you to lead them away to safety."

"I thought it was safe here," Ned said.

Debbie didn't answer.

"Ned, I'm your mother and I'm ordering you to — "

"You can give all the orders you want. I'm not abandoning you here."

"Nick and Kia need you."

"No we don't," I said.

Everybody looked at me in disbelief. "You

think you can find your way out of here alone?" Kia asked.

"Of course not. It's just that Ned isn't going to leave his mother and neither are we."

"I agree," Kia said.

"But you have to!" Debbie protested.

"We're not going anywhere without you," Ned said. He sounded calm and in control. "And you can yell at me all you want. It isn't going to change anything. I'm not leaving you here."

"Correction," Kia said. "*We're* not leaving you here. Period. End of discussion."

"Look, I don't want to argue — "

"There's no point in arguing," Ned said, cutting his mother off.

"I just want you to know — all of you to know — just how serious this is," she said.

"We know it's serious," I said.

"I don't think you do. We're in danger, real danger. I think we'll be okay but there are no guarantees. Fires are unpredictable. We could get caught up in it. We could . . . we could — "

"Die?" I asked.

She nodded her head.

I took a deep breath. "I know. We all know."

"You should all get out of here while you still have a chance," Debbie said.

"Maybe we should," Ned said, "but we're not going to."

"We're not going anywhere," Kia added.

"We're all staying together," I said.

Debbie didn't answer right away. She looked like she was thinking through what she was going to say next.

"None of you are going to listen to me, are you?" she finally asked.

"We'll listen to you," Ned said. "We just aren't going to leave you. What should we do now?"

"There's nothing much we can do," she said. "We have to wait . . . although this probably isn't the best spot to wait."

"What do you mean?" I asked.

"We need to find the most open piece of ground we can find, away from trees and bush, preferably close to water."

"Like the basketball court," Kia said.

"The basketball court would be perfect," Debbie said, "except it's pretty far from here."

"It's not that far. It can't be much more than a kilometer," I said.

"There's no way I can walk that far. I can barely stand."

"Don't worry. You won't have to walk," Ned said.

"I need to stop," I said.

"Me too," Ned agreed.

Gently we lowered the branches, setting Debbie down on the ground. She was lying on a rough-made sling that Ned had built out of two long branches and a cover from one of the seats of the truck. The cover was strung between the two long poles, one on each side. Ned and I each held the end of one of the poles while the other end dragged along in the dirt. It was hard work — incredibly hard work — but we were making progress, dragging her along the road toward the spot where the trail led down to the court.

Kia was carrying the three cages holding the animals. They weren't as heavy as dragging Debbie, but they were pretty awkward to carry.

While Ned had been building the sling, both Kia and I had been working too. Debbie had insisted that she wasn't leaving all the family pictures behind in the truck. She had us put all the photo albums in a big blue plastic box, snap the lid shut and then *bury* it. She said that even if the fire passed this way it would still survive.

Ned was looking back in the direction we'd just come from. I turned around and was shocked by the sight. The whole sky was now black with smoke.

"It's moving fast, isn't it?" I said, although I was less asking a question than stating the obvious.

"Fast."

"Are we moving faster than it?"

He shook his head. "I don't know . . . I can't tell."

"Then maybe we better get moving again." I stood up and Ned got to his feet too.

"Lift on three," Ned said.

I grabbed one branch and he grabbed the second.

"One . . . two . . . and three."

I strained under the weight but we lifted Debbie off the ground. We started moving again.

"You want to trade?" Kia said.

"Maybe in a while," I replied.

"I feel so bad," Debbie said. "Maybe I could get up and limp along for a while again."

"You just stay right there!" Kia warned her. "We can move faster this way."

Debbie had tried to walk before and we had actually moved *slower*.

"We'll get there," I said, more to myself

than Debbie. It was hard, and she was heavy, but somehow having a fire coming up through the forest behind gave me a burst of energy.

We set the sling down for the last time under the tree that held one of the nets. The last part of the trip, through the berry bushes, had been downhill, so the going had been a little bit easier.

There was now more than just the smell of smoke; there was a faint haze that hovered in the air.

"I need something to drink," Kia said. She'd placed the three cages in the middle of the court.

We walked over to the little creek. The court still looked good, though the corner beside the creek had been further eroded by the rush of water during the storm. The creek had receded somewhat, but it was still much higher than normal. I stopped at the water's edge, bent down and cupped my hands to get a drink. The water was freezing cold and delicious as it slid down my throat. I didn't think I'd ever tasted anything as good.

Kia waded into the water. She stopped when it was knee-deep on her. That looked like a good idea. I stepped in and the cold, clear water surrounded me. I splashed the water up onto my face and arms.

I looked back at the scene. Ned was sitting beside his mother at the edge of the court. Behind them, the hill sloping up was filled with small bushes. Behind that, the sky was dark, filled with thick black clouds of smoke rising up out of the trees. I looked over my shoulder. Beyond the creek the cliff was steep and rocky and covered with moss and grass and shrubs and stunted trees. There wasn't much to burn, so the cliff protected us from that direction. Protected us and trapped us.

"You scared?" Kia asked.

"What do you think?"

"Me too," she said. "I guess there's nothing to do but wait."

"I hate waiting. I just hate it!" I snapped.

"I know," she said, nodding her head. "You always want to get the game started."

I scoffed. "The game . . . think about all the times we've stood on the sidelines of a basketball court, about all the games we've played and how important we thought they were. How we'd spend all that time thinking about the game, worrying, losing sleep — "

"How *you'd* lose sleep," Kia said, cutting me off.

"Fine, how *I'd* lose sleep," I agreed. Kia could always sleep. "But you can't tell me that you didn't think that whatever game we were getting ready to play was the most important thing in the world."

She shrugged, but didn't disagree.

"And I think about how crucial every shot seemed. Do or *die* plays. Sudden *death* overtime. And now look around."

I scanned the scene surrounding us. The air was becoming more smoke filled and I thought that I could even see the glare of flames in the distance.

"We're going to be okay, Nick."

I looked over at her. "You know, I think you're right. At least I want to believe you're right." I paused. "This is real. Makes all those basketball games seem pretty unimportant, doesn't it?"

"I guess it does," she admitted.

We waded out of the water and flopped down on the dusty shore.

"My father always says that the best thing about sports is that it prepares you for difficult times, teaches you life lessons," I said. "I can't figure out how anything I was ever taught on a court could help me here . . . can you?"

Kia didn't answer.

"I can't think of how a good hook shot would help right now," I said.

"It would be nice to have a team here now." Kia said. "At least a team of firefighters."

"They'd know what to do. They'd have a plan and plays, just like a team," I agreed.

"And I bet they have a leader, a guy like a coach or captain, who tells everybody what they have to do and how to do it," Kia added.

"That would be the fire chief . . . they must have a fire chief. The people on the team don't just go and do whatever they want."

"It won't be that long until the firefighters are here," Kia said. "It's been almost three hours since Debbie radioed in, and they said they'd be here in six hours, so that means that they'll be here in less then three hours."

"That was before we reported the second fire — and that's if the radio was even working after the crash — so they have to fight their way through the first fire and then get through the landslide and — "

"I get the idea," Kia said. "It could be a lot longer. If only we had somebody who could tell us what to do and then we could do it."

I looked up to where Ned sat with his mother. "Maybe we do," I said softly. "Maybe we do."

Chapter Twelve

"I've read lots of books about forest fires," Ned admitted, "but I've never even been near one before."

"But you know how to fight them, right?" Kia asked. "You know what to do."

"I know the principles and practices of forest fires and their management and control."

"What?" Kia asked.

"He knows what to do," I said.

"We both know what to do," Debbie said. "You don't live with a park ranger all those years without picking up a few things, but it's not practical for us to even think about putting out this fire."

"I'm not thinking about putting anything out," I said. "I just want to know what we can do to protect ourselves until the real fighters come."

"Couldn't we go in the water and just keep our heads above the water?" Kia asked. "The water can't burn."

"You wouldn't burn, but you could suffocate," Ned said.

"Suffocate?"

"Have no air to breathe. The fire doesn't just burn wood. It uses the air as fuel too. It draws off all the oxygen and leaves just smoke and gases that we can't breathe."

That sounded awful. A shiver went through my entire body.

"There has to be something that we can do," Kia said. "What would real firefighters do if they were here with us right now? Would they be sitting around, doing nothing?"

"No, of course not," Ned said. "They'd be making a firebreak at least."

"That's right . . . you mentioned that to me when we were hiking . . . that's what the tools were for."

"What's a firebreak?" Kia asked.

"A firebreak is also known as a fire line or a fireguard and — "

"We don't care what the different names are!" I snapped. "Just tell us *what* it is!"

"A firebreak is a place in the forest, like a long line, where there's nothing for the fire to burn, just open ground, and when the fire hits that line it stops because it has no more fuel."

"And how do you make a firebreak?" I asked.

"Often they use a technique involving a backfire and a bulldozer to clear away enough — "

"You and your father didn't bring a bulldozer on you when we went on that hike," I said.

"It doesn't have to be a bulldozer," Ned protested. "You can make a break with rakes and shovels and a chainsaw."

"And you have all of that stuff back at your house, right?" Kia asked.

Ned nodded.

I looked around at the court. The back was protected by the creek and cliff.

"The water and rocks are a firebreak, aren't they?" I asked.

Again Ned nodded.

"So we're protected from that side. Could we build a firebreak on the other three sides?" I asked.

"That would be no problem for a squad of firefighters."

"That wasn't what I asked!"

"I . . . I don't know . . . but we could try."

"That's all I wanted to hear. Then let's try."

There was a loud "bang" and I jumped into the air.

"What was that?" I demanded.

"A tree exploding," Ned said. "The fire superheats all the sap and then the top sort of blows off."

"Is that dangerous?"

"Very."

We moved up the road toward their house. Kia had stayed behind to watch Debbie and the animals. Two of us could carry all the things we'd need.

It was an eerie feeling moving up the road and away from the relative safety of the basketball court. It was strange. We were walking toward a fire, knowing that another fire was moving in from behind us as well.

As we moved up the road the smoke became thicker. I could taste it in my mouth. And there was a sound, sort of like the wind but different . . . more like a "whooshing" sort of noise.

"What is that sound?" I asked.

"That's the fire. It's not far from here now."

That wasn't what I wanted to hear. "How much farther is your house?" It seemed like we'd walked for a lot longer than I thought we should have.

"Not far now. We should be able to see it when we reach the top of this hill."

I remembered when we first arrived and Debbie stopped the truck right up there and we had our first look at the house, partially hidden, nestled in among the trees. It all looked so peaceful. What was it going to look like now? I took a deep breath, closed my eyes and prepared myself for the worst.

"Oh my goodness," Ned gasped.

My eyes popped open. It looked like the whole horizon was on fire! There was a wall of flames in the distance shooting up into the blackened sky.

"We have to . . . have to go back," I sputtered.

"We still have time."

"But you told me how fast a fire can travel."

"It can only travel fast if there's a strong wind, and there's almost no wind," Ned explained.

"I do feel some wind," I said. "But it feels like it's blowing *toward* the fire."

"That's not wind."

"If it's not the wind then what is it?" I asked.

"Remember when I mentioned that fires use up air."

"Yeah?"

"The oxygen that's being burned by the fire has to be replaced. It sucks in air from the area surrounding the fire. That's what you feel."

"And you're sure we have time?" I asked again.

"We do . . . but let's move faster anyway."

We rushed down the hill and circled around the side of the house to the toolshed. The house blocked out my view of the fire, and if it hadn't been for the foul, burning smell it would have seemed like there wasn't even a fire there.

Ned opened up the shed and started pulling things off the shelves and hooks.

"Here, take these," he said, handing me two rakes and a shovel. "Can you carry more?"

"I can carry half of whatever needs to be carried."

He handed me another shovel and pulled down a chainsaw, laying it on the floor of the shed. Next he grabbed a big can of gas. He handed it to me. It was heavy. Somehow it didn't seem like a great idea to have anything flammable around, but I knew he'd need that to power the chainsaw. He then grabbed a large round container with a nozzle on the front. It looked sort of like another gasoline can, but different.

Ned slung the chainsaw over his shoulder, picked up the strange container in one hand and an axe in the other.

"Since I don't see a bulldozer, I guess this will have to do. Let's get going."

Kia went first with the rake. She was pushing before her anything that was loose . . . leaves, pine needles, branches. It was amazing how much stuff littered the forest floor.

I followed behind with my shovel. What she couldn't rake, I tried to dig out. Tufts of grass, plants, small bushes — some of those I just grabbed and ripped out of the ground. Then Ned followed me. He was using the axe or chainsaw to cut down whatever couldn't be raked or ripped out of the ground. He cut the tops off with the chainsaw and then took the axe and chopped off the last little bit standing above ground. I couldn't imagine my mother even letting me hold a chainsaw. But of course it was different with Ned. He'd grown up in the bush and he knew exactly what he was doing.

I stopped and looked back at what we'd done. In thirty minutes we'd managed to clear a whole five-foot-wide line — actually a whole semicircle around the court, touching the creek on both sides. On the other side of the fire- break the bushes, grass, leaves and pine needles were starting to accumulate into a long pile, parallel to the break.

Debbie hobbled over. Her leg was looking more swollen and the expression on her face left no doubt how painful each attempt to put weight on her leg must be.

"You're all doing a wonderful job!" she said. "I just wish I could do something to help."

"Does this look alright, what we're doing?" Kia asked.

"It looks fine," she said. "Ned?"

He nodded his head. "Just like the diagram in the book, except the open space needs to be bigger, wider."

"How much wider?" I asked. This had taken a tremendous amount of work and I was feeling tired and hot. It wasn't just that the midday sun was shining down on us, but I thought the wind was hot . . . much hotter than it would have been if there wasn't a fire.

"It has to be a lot wider. Ideally we need between fifty and a hundred feet," he said.

"We can never clear that much space!" Kia said. "Never!"

"She's right, Ned. It would take days."

"And we don't have days. Look how much closer the fire's moved."

She was right. Looking up the slope there were places where the road was already blocked from view by the smoke and flames. It looked like the two fires, one moving from the south and the other from the north, had met right across from us. We were now locked into a circle in the center — a center that was becoming smaller and smaller and –

"Look!" I screamed in shock as a deer — no, two deer, three, four — leaped across the road and thundered down the slope, dodging around the bushes, heading straight toward us! At the last second they cut off to the side and ran into the water, coming to a stop in the middle of the small creek. All four just froze there, their mouths open, panting, the only movement being their chests heaving up and down.

"I hadn't even thought of all the animals," Kia said. "Where have they all gone?"

"Those that can run have taken off," Ned

said. "Others have just . . . have just . . . "
he let his sentence trail off and he looked
toward the ground. There was no doubt
what he was trying to say.

The deer continued to stand there, staring
up at the fire, ignoring us as if we weren't
even there.

"I've read about this sort of thing happening,"
Ned said. "It was written by a smoke jumper
in Alaska who witnessed a deer and a cougar,
practically standing side by side, watching
the fire and not even bothering with one
another. Isn't that fascinating?"

"Yeah, right, but you were saying you
knew what to do next . . . how to clear the
rest of the firebreak."

"Oh yeah, right."

"What can we do to help?" Kia asked.

"Nothing. There's nothing you can do.
Maybe you two should just go and get a
drink . . . wet down your clothes . . . help
my mother get a drink. I'll take care of
things."

"Okay, sure," I said.

I dragged myself toward the stream. My
legs felt heavy and I was having to work to
draw in a full breath. Between the smoke
and the heat and dust and hard work I felt

exhausted. I collapsed beside the creek, splashing water into my face.

Kia had gone over and helped Debbie to her feet. I felt badly. I should have helped too. I tried to stand up and my legs just gave way and I fell back down. Debbie, her arm around Kia's shoulders, limped over, and the two of them slumped to the ground beside me.

"I'm sorry," I muttered. "I wanted to help, but I'm just so tired."

"You all must be exhausted," Debbie said. "And I'm the one who should be sorry."

"Sorry for what?" Kia asked.

"For not being able to help and — "

"That's not your fault, you're hurt," Kia said.

"And for getting hurt. If I'd been driving more carefully the accident wouldn't have happened."

"That wasn't your fault either," I said. "You couldn't know about the landslide, and it was just there when we turned the corner."

"You're both being kind," Debbie said. "Kind and brave. You've *all* been so brave, so *magnificent*."

"Magnificent," Kia said, nodding her head. "That just about sums me up to a T."

Despite myself, despite everything, I started

146

to laugh and both Debbie and Kia joined in. Ned turned around. He looked at us like we were all insane. Maybe we were.

"Do you know, I was really worried about Ned having to start school. I wondered how he'd get along, if he could handle it."

"He's going to have some friends to help him," I said.

"He's already *had* some friends help him . . . the two of you."

"But he's going to have three friends at his new school, three kids on the Salmon Arm travel team, three kids who really, really want him to play on their team."

"That's all great, and I guess there's no doubt that we're moving now."

"There isn't?" I asked.

"Think about it, Nick," Kia said.

Then it hit me. They didn't even have a house anymore. The fire must have swept over their home. And the truck in the other direction. All that was left were some buried photo albums, the animals, and the tools we'd taken from the shed.

"None of that matters," Debbie said. "I've never cared much about stuff anyway. All that matters is that we're going to get out of here."

"What's Ned doing?" Kia asked.

I was wondering the same thing. He'd been walking along the edge of the firebreak, holding onto that strange can thing he'd brought from the shed.

"He's going to set the brush on fire," Debbie said.

"He's going to what?" I asked, hearing the words but not believing what she'd said.

"He's going to set the brush on fire," she repeated.

"But that's crazy!" Kia exclaimed. "We don't need any more fire, we need *less* fire!"

I tried to get to my feet but I stumbled, almost toppling over before I regained my footing.

"Ned, stop!" I screamed as I got up and stumbled toward him.

"It's okay!" I heard Debbie yell from behind me.

"What are you doing?" I demanded.

"I'm starting a backfire."

"Why would you want to start a fire?" I questioned.

"I don't have any choice. We have to clear more space, make the firebreak wider, and this is the only way to do that," he explained.

"So . . . to save us from the fire you're going to make a fire?" I asked. That made no sense.

"Exactly. I'm going to set a fire and it will burn away from us, using up all the fuel the big fire would use and clearing out a firebreak that will protect us. It's called a controlled fire."

"And this will work?"

"This is what forest firefighters do. I've read all about it."

"But, can you do it?"

Ned didn't answer.

"Ned . . . can you do it?"

"I can try . . . if you think I should."

The whole idea seemed nuts. We were surrounded by a forest fire, hiding in the last little spot that wasn't aflame, and Ned wanted to deliberately set another fire right by us.

I took a deep breath. "This is the thing that's supposed to be done, right?"

Ned nodded his head.

I reached over and put a hand on his shoulder. "Then you do it."

Ned smiled. "You better get back," he said.

I gladly retreated away from him. Ned pulled out a book of matches and lit a little flame that glowed on the top of the can. He then hit a switch and a line of fire leapt out toward the loose bush and pine needles, setting them on fire! He walked along the line, doing the same thing over and over and over, until the entire edge of the firebreak was on fire.

From where I stood I could feel the heat thrown off by the fire. I stepped farther back and shielded my eyes from the bright glare.

"And me without any marshmallows," Kia said. She was standing just behind me.

Ned came over. "Now grab your shovels and rakes. We walk behind the fire and anything that isn't burned after the fire passes we have to dig up or bury. There has to be nothing left that can burn."

I wasn't sure if I even had the strength to walk back and pick up my shovel. I was exhausted — more exhausted than I'd ever been in my life. And scared — more scared than I'd ever been in my life.

"Come on, Kia," I said as I started off for the shovels. Scared was more powerful than exhausted.

Chapter Thirteen

It was the most unbelievable sight I had ever seen in my whole life. The entire forest was on fire . . . reds and oranges racing up the trees, leaping for the sky, finally replaced by a thick curtain of smoke that blackened the sky and practically blotted out the sun — it was only a dim light in the sky. Although the closest part of the fire was at least a hundred feet away, I could feel the heat against my cheeks.

That was as close as the fire could come. We were protected by an open, bare and burnt section — the firebreak. I don't know what would have happened if it wasn't for that open space . . . actually I did know and I didn't want to even think about it.

I slipped farther into the water. We were all lying in the water, only our shoulders and heads on the sandy bank of the creek. The four of us were sharing the same space with the four deer, no more than a dozen feet away, all of us staring at the fire. All of us except Kia. She lay on her back, staring straight up at the little spot of blue sky that still survived above our heads.

Ned started coughing again — coughing badly — and Debbie had him take another sip of water. The smoke was bad, twirling and swirling all around us, but hadn't sealed us in completely . . . at least not yet.

"You okay?" I asked Ned.

He nodded.

"They won't be much longer," I said.

"Who?"

"The firefighters. It's been more than six hours. They'll be here soon." I paused. "Right?"

"I don't know," he said. "I don't know how big the fire is, how far it extends out in all directions. They won't even know to look for us here."

He was right. I just wished that he wasn't right. Or at least that he hadn't told me. Hope was about the only thing I had to hang on to.

I closed my eyes. I didn't want to look at the fire. I wanted to just pretend that I wasn't here, that none of us were here, that none of this was happening.

I thought about my house, about my mother and father. I wanted to be home, safe in my bed, my parents downstairs to take care of me. All I had to do was call and they'd come running up the stairs to make everything right again. It gave me a warm feeling.

I opened my eyes and came back to reality. Even with them closed, I couldn't get away from the smoke or the sound. The sound was something I hadn't even thought about, but it was inescapable.

There was the constant roar of the flames, but there was also popping and buzzing, the sound of trees crashing as they toppled over or exploded into flames or . . . what was that sound? It was different. High pitched and constant. Almost like an engine . . . an engine!

I pushed myself up onto my elbows, then stood up.

"What is it?" Kia demanded as she rose to her knees. "What's wrong?"

"Ssshhhh!" I hissed at her.

I walked out of the water and a few feet away from the creek. I could feel the heat of the fire, and the smoke was thicker at head height than it had been along the ground. I turned my head to the side to try to listen, to pick up the sound again. Had I just been imagining it, or was it just another sound made by the fire itself? Maybe it had all been in my head instead of my ears. I was imagining it because I wanted to hear something so badly and — no . . . there it was again, the sound of an engine! Was it a chainsaw or a truck or a — an airplane! It swooped low over the trees, punching out through the smoke, a blue and yellow blur, driven along by the two spinning propellers I'd heard.

"We're here!" I screamed as I ran across the clearing, waving my arms in the air as it vanished from view and the sound of the engines faded and then disappeared completely.

I spun around to where everybody was lying in the water. "Did you see it?" I yelled. "Did you see it?"

More importantly, did the plane see us?

Then the sound of the engines could be heard again, and it was getting louder and louder . . . they'd seen us, they were circling back!

"It saw us!" I screamed. "We're saved!"

Ned suddenly got to his feet and started running toward me. He was screaming something but I couldn't make out the words over the sound of the fire and the plane — the plane! I started jumping up and down and waving my arms.

"We're here!" I yelled. "We're he — " I was hit from behind and I staggered and then tumbled to the ground. Ned had tackled me and had his arms wrapped around my legs!

"What are you doing?" I screamed out as I tried to get back on my feet.

"Lie flat, put your head down!" Ned yelled and then lunged forward, pushing my face into the ground!

I struggled to right myself when I was smashed into the ground, the air forced out of my lungs, my whole body feeling like it had been punched and pressed into the dirt! It felt like I'd been hit by an elephant. I pushed myself up on one arm and strained, struggled to try and draw my breath . . . I gasped and air rushed into my collapsed lungs. I was soaking wet! I spat, trying to get rid of dirt that had been driven into my mouth and throat.

"What . . . what . . . what happened?" I sputtered.

Ned's glasses were missing, he was completely covered with dirt and his hair was plastered down to his head. He opened his mouth to talk and I could tell by the panicked look on his face that he couldn't get air either. A shudder went through his entire body.

"Bomb," he hissed, the word just barely escaping.

"They dropped a bomb on us?" That was what it felt like, but why would they bomb us?

"Bomber . . . water bomber . . . they dropped water on us," he said.

I looked around. The ground was soaked and

there were puddles. There was a sizzling sound and clouds of smoke — no steam — were rising from the trees closest to us . . . they weren't on fire anymore . . . they were steaming.

Then my attention was caught by movement. I looked over. There was a fish — no, *two* fish — flipping and flopping on the ground right beside me.

"Fish," I said to Ned in amazement, "there are fish."

"They were scooped up by the water bomber when it filled its tanks. Sometimes they get fish or ducks or driftwood."

"Is that what hit me . . . hit us . . . a log?"

He shook his head. "Just water. Thousands and thousands of gallons of water. But if you'd been standing up it could have killed you."

"Why did they drop it on us?"

"Probably couldn't see us. They're just attacking the fire."

I suddenly heard the sound of another engine. The plane was coming back to drop more water!

"The plane's coming back. We've got to move before it hits us again!" I shouted.

I struggled to get to my feet, but Ned just held on to me. Between his size and my exhaustion I couldn't budge.

"We're okay," Ned said. "It isn't the plane."

I looked up into the sky and saw — a helicopter! Its two gigantic rotors spun around and around as it came in and then hovered above the center of the clearing. I brought up my hands to shield my eyes from the dirt and ashes swirling around and hitting me in the face, but nothing could protect me from the sound. It was an incredible racket.

"Look!" Ned yelled over the roar.

The big side door of the helicopter slid open and I could see people standing there, and then ropes — one, two, half a dozen — dropped out. And then a man started down one of the lines, rappelling toward the ground. He was followed by a second man, and a third, until every one of the lines was filled by somebody.

"Rap Attack firefighting team," Ned said.

I didn't know what to say or think. I sat there and watched as the men glided down the ropes, touching down on the ground. No sooner had they landed than they grabbed shovels and axes from their big backpacks and began attacking the edge of the fire.

"Now it's over," Ned said. "We're safe."

They'd driven us to the airport in their brand- new, shiny, four-wheel-drive SUV — complete with air conditioning! Apparently they couldn't get a truck that didn't have air conditioning.

"I miss the old truck," Ned said.

"It's still there in the ditch — at least what's left of it — so maybe I can take you to visit it sometime," Dan joked.

We'd spent the last few days living with them in their new house . . . a rental on the outskirts of Salmon Arm. Dan complained about how he didn't know if he could get used to "city living." Considering that their nearest neighbor was half a kilometer down the road, I didn't think that was much of a problem.

"I'm so glad you two came," Ned said.

"Us too. It was a real experience," I replied.

"Almost too much of an experience," Kia added.

"You know the strangest part?" Ned asked.

"I can think of dozens of things that happened that could be the strangest part. Which one are you referring to?" I questioned.

"I was scared that you two would be really bored when you came to visit."

Chapter Fourteen

"We're going to miss you both so much!" Debbie gushed as she gave first Kia, and then me, a big hug. She had her crutches tucked under her arms. The lower half of her leg was in a cast.

"We're going to miss you too," I said.

"We're going to miss *everybody*," Kia added.

Ned and Dan both smiled.

"And you have everything?" Debbie asked.

"Everything that was left," Kia said.

"Oh . . . of course . . . what am I thinking?" Debbie replied.

Most of our clothes and things had been destroyed when the house was burned down, and the few things we'd packed into the truck were lost when the truck had been burned to a crisp as well.

"That's okay. We didn't lose anything that can't be replaced," I said.

"That's what I keep saying as well," Dan agreed. "Starting with that beat-up old truck."

Both Kia and I broke into laughter and Ned gave a big smile.

"A little more boredom would have suited me just fine," Kia said.

"Maybe you can arrange for things to be more boring next summer," I suggested.

"Next summer?"

"Yeah. Kia and I were talking about how it would be good to come back next year . . . that is if we're invited."

"Of course you're invited!" Ned exclaimed. "They can come back, right, Mom, right, Dad?"

"No question," Debbie said.

"No problem," Dan added. "We'd love to have you back, and this time you should come for longer, as long as you want, maybe even the whole summer!"

"Thanks," I said.

"Kia, Nick?"

I turned around. It was the flight attendant.

"I'm afraid it's time to go. You'll have to say your last good-byes."

Kia gave Debbie and then Ned and Dan a great big hug. I hugged Debbie and then shook hands with Dan.

"Thanks," Ned said as we finally shook hands.

"Thank you for inviting us."

"I wasn't thanking you for coming," he said. "I was thanking you for everything else."

"Thanking me? You're the one who saved the day. I don't even want to think what would have happened if you weren't there."

"It wasn't me," Ned said. "It was us, all of us. We make a good team, don't we?"

"Not a good team . . . a great team."

Ned wrapped his arms around me and gave me a great big hug. I hugged him back.

"See you next summer, cousin."

"Next summer."

Kia and I walked off with the flight attendant. We turned around and waved just before we ducked through a corridor leading to the plane.

"Are you two still nervous about having a pilot named Crash?" the flight attendant asked as we neared the door to the plane.

"I was never nervous," Kia replied.

"And you?" she asked me.

I shook my head. "Not anymore. I just have one question."

"What's that?"

"Does this Crash guy ever fly water bombers?"